NIGHT OF THE WEREWOLF

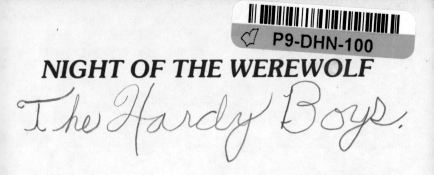

The Hardy Boys.

THE HARDY BOYS® MYSTERY STORIES

NIGHT OF THE WEREWOLF

Franklin W. Dixon

Illustrated by
Leslie Morrill

WANDERER BOOKS
New York

Manufactured in the United States of America

10 9 8 7 6 5

Wanderer and colophon are trademarks of Simon & Schuster

THE HARDY BOYS is a trademark of Stratemeyer Syndicate,
registered in the United States Patent and Trademark Office.

Library of Congress Cataloging in Publication Data

Dixon, Franklin W
Night of the werewolf.

(Hardy boys mystery stories; 59)
SUMMARY: When a ferocious, wolf-like creature appears in a
small town, the Hardy boys are engaged to clear the name of a
young man who has a history of werewolves in his family.
[1. Werewolves—Fiction.   2. Mystery and detective stories]
I. Title.
PZ7.D644Ni   [Fic]   79-17046

ISBN 0-671-95498-9
ISBN 0-671-95520-9 pbk.

Contents

1

The Glowing Beast

"Oh, oh! Look who's here," said Frank Hardy. "Mountain Man himself."

"Man Mountain, you mean," quipped his brother, Joe.

It was Saturday evening, and the Hardys were munching pizzas in the Bayport Diner with their dates, Callie Shaw and Iola Morton. Iola's tubby brother Chet and lanky Biff Hooper had just walked in and came to their table.

"Boy, you've got to see that scene where Lobo Jack fights a bear on the edge of a cliff!" Chet exclaimed, his moonface alight with excitement.

"Don't tell me you saw that movie about the Rocky Mountain trappers again!" Joe groaned and the girls giggled. "What is this, the tenth time?"

Before Chet could bore them with more breathless scenes, the Hardys paid their bill and the group left. They were halfway across the parking lot when Iola gasped in fear.

"Good grief! What's that?"

The Bayport Diner lay on the edge of town and was bordered by a patch of woods. Iola pointed to a weird-looking creature bounding out from among the trees. *It was a snarling, wolflike beast whose fur glowed in the dark!*

"Watch out!" Frank cried. "That critter means business!"

Callie screamed in alarm as she saw the animal charging straight toward them, its fangs bared ferociously. The beast would be upon them before they could either reach the safety of the Hardys' car or retreat into the diner!

"Get behind us!" Joe shouted to the girls; then he and Frank thrust out their arms to fend off the expected attack.

Luckily Callie's scream had been heard and their plight seen from inside the diner. Chet, Biff, and several others dashed out to help.

"Beat it, you!" Biff bellowed, and the others joined in the outcry, yelling and waving their arms.

The glowing wolf-creature stopped short with a deep-throated growl, evidently startled by the noisy outburst from the young people. Then it turned and ran back into the woods.

"Wow! My legs were ready to give way," Iola confessed, clinging to Joe's arm. She and Callie were both pale with fright.

"What *was* that thing?" Chet asked as he hurried up to them.

"I've no idea," said Frank, "but I sure intend to find out."

He and Joe picked up flashlights from their car and were about to head into the woods when Callie called out anxiously, "Wait! Where are you going?"

"That brute could be dangerous!" a man from the diner added.

"Don't worry, we'll keep our distance," Joe replied. "We just want to see where it came from."

Blond, seventeen-year-old Joe Hardy and his dark-haired older brother, Frank, were the sons of famed private detective Fenton Hardy, who had once been a crack investigator on the New York City police force.

The two young sleuths never could resist a mystery, and the weird creature who had come streaking out of the darkness at them posed too great a challenge to pass up. Their father had taught them never to take foolish chances, but they felt the glare of their flashlight beams away from the diner would dazzle their quarry enough to keep it from attacking.

The phantom beast had disappeared among the trees and underbrush. Cautiously, the Hardys pressed forward, moving their flashlights to and fro and keeping their eyes peeled for a glimpse of its glowing fur.

4

"Maybe it veered off in a different direction," Joe conjectured.

"No, it went this way," Frank said. "Look at this freshly broken shrubbery. The stalks are still moist."

"But how could it vanish so fast? That fur alone would give it away at quite a distance."

"I know. I can't figure it out, either. If we found any of its hairs that brushed off on trees around here, we could take them back to the lab and examine them under a microscope."

"That's an idea! It might give us a clue to—," Joe broke off as his brother raised a hand for silence.

"Sounds like Chet calling us," said the older Hardy boy. The two listened.

Sure enough, their friend's yell from the parking lot was repeated. "Come back here, Frank and Joe!"

The Hardys retreated through the woods in the direction of the diner. Chet was leaning against their car with Biff and the girls standing next to him.

"What's up?" Frank asked.

"You got a radio call." Chet pointed to a red light blinking on the dashboard.

Frank opened the door and slipped behind the wheel. He flicked a switch on the specially licensed radio transceiver mounted under their instrument panel.

"H-1 here," he spoke into the hand mike. "Come in, please."

"G calling," crackled a voice from the speaker. "Do you read me?"

5

"Loud and clear, Aunt Gertrude. Anything wrong?"

"Yes. Customer's here and no one's minding the store."

"Customer? You mean a client?"

"Do I have to spell it out?" his aunt replied tartly.

"Must be a new case for Dad," murmured Joe, who was standing at the car door, listening in.

"Who is it, Aunt Gertrude?" Frank inquired into the mike. "Any idea what the problem is?"

"Come home and find out," was the withering response. "I know better than to discuss cases over the air, and so should you!"

"Right you are, Aunty." Frank chuckled wryly.

"As always," Joe muttered with a grin.

"We'll start back as soon as we take the girls home," Frank added and signed off.

"We can drop Callie off if it's something urgent," Chet offered.

"Of course they can, and don't worry about it," Iola said with an understanding smile as Joe started to apologize for ending the evening so abruptly.

Both the cute, pixie-faced girl and blonde, brown-eyed Callie Shaw, who was Frank's date, said good-by to the Hardys and walked off with Biff and Chet.

"Something should be done about that wolf-dog, or whatever it was," Frank said with a worried frown before starting the car.

Nick Pappadopolos, the shirt-sleeved proprietor of the diner, who had been talking to several people in

6

the parking lot, walked up to the group and overheard the remark.

"I'll take care of it," he promised. "I'll call the pound and tell 'em there's a dangerous animal loose. Who knows, it may even be rabid!"

"Thanks, Nick." Frank waved and backed out of the lot.

They were almost home when Joe said, "Frank, you forgot your jacket in the diner."

"I thought I left it in the back seat."

Joe squirmed around to look. "It's not there. You must have forgotten it."

Frank hesitated for a moment. Should he drive back and get his coat? He decided it was more important to meet the client who was waiting for them. "I'll pick it up tomorrow," he said and drove straight home.

A small red station wagon was parked in front of their white frame house on Elm Street. The boys scrutinized it quickly on their way to the garage.

Somewhat to their surprise, the unknown client turned out to be an attractive, though rather plump, teenage girl named Alena Tabor. She had curly brown hair and a fresh, apple-cheeked face.

"I didn't mean to call at such a late hour," she explained, "but I had car trouble on the way to Bayport."

"That's a shame," said Joe. "Can we help?"

"Thanks, it's fixed now. Just a broken fan belt, but it took hours getting road service."

7

"And now that you're here, Dad's away. I'm sorry about that," Frank said politely. "Is there anything we can do? Joe and I sometimes assist him on his cases."

"I know, and you also investigate mysteries on your own, which is why I'm here." Alena smiled. "Actually, you two are the ones I came to see. I'm the daughter of Karel Tabor."

"The architect!" Joe exclaimed, recognizing the name. "I believe Dad interviewed him recently."

Alena nodded. "Yes, in connection with that case Mr. Hardy's working on for the insurance underwriters. So we knew he would be busy. But my father thought you might help us with our problem."

"We'll sure try," Frank said. "What *is* your problem?"

"Werewolves."

The Hardys were startled. They stared at her, wide-eyed, as if not quite sure they had heard her correctly.

"You did say werewolves, didn't you?" Joe inquired.

Alena smiled. "I know, you probably think I'm crazy. But it so happens there's a tradition of werewolves in our family."

"Tell us about it," Frank said.

Alena related that the Tabors were descended from a Bohemian soldier—a native of what is now Czechoslovakia—who had come to the United States in Revolutionary War days. He had deserted from King George's hired Hessian troops, joined Washington's army, and later settled in the Mohawk Valley in northern New York.

8

"We still live up that way," Alena added, "in the Adirondack Mountains near Hawk River."

Joe looked puzzled. "From what Dad said, I thought your father's office was in New York City."

"It is. He commutes there every day by helicopter," Alena explained.

She said that her twenty-four-year-old brother John was also an architect and had recently graduated from college. A brilliant student, his building designs had won prizes in several competitions, and he expected to join their father's firm.

"But then he suffered a nervous breakdown from overwork," Alena went on unhappily, "and now we're wondering if he's going out of his mind."

Frank frowned. "What gave you that idea?"

"The family legend. It says that every seventh generation, some member of the Tabor family becomes a werewolf." She glanced nervously at the Hardys. "You know what a werewolf is, of course?"

"According to superstition, it's a human being who turns into a wolf, usually during the full moon every month," Joe said.

"That's right," Alena said. "And my brother and I are the seventh generation since the last reported werewolf in the Tabor family."

"You don't believe such yarns, do you?" Frank asked.

Alena shivered. "I don't know what to believe! Lately John has been behaving very strangely. And now there are stories about some awful creature

9

attacking people and livestock around Hawk River during the full moon—supposedly a werewolf with luminous fur that glows in the dark!"

"Fiddlesticks!" said Aunt Gertrude, who had been hovering in the living room after serving the young people cocoa. "Some local busybodies have probably heard of your family legend, dear."

Alena shook her head. "That's just it, they *haven't* heard it yet. We never talked about it in public. But Father mentioned it once to a magazine writer who was interviewing him. Now we're afraid someone may dig up that story."

"What exactly do you want us to do?" Joe asked.

Alena said her family owned a small cottage near Hawk River. She suggested that the Hardys drive up to the Adirondacks on Monday, bringing friends if they liked, and stay there during the ensuing full-moon period. By posing as vacationers, they could keep an eye on the situation without attracting attention or causing any gossip.

"Sounds like a great idea. We'll enjoy it," Frank said, and Joe agreed.

Just as Alena was leaving, weird howls echoed outside the house. Frank saw a look of fear pass over the girl's face. He told her to wait in the hall while he and Joe searched the area with flashlights.

Soon the boys returned. "Don't worry, no lurking werewolves," Joe reported. "Come on, we'll walk you to your car."

10

Alena smiled with relief. A few minutes later, she drove off and the boys returned to the house. Frank switched on the electronic alarm system before everyone settled down for the night.

"What do you make of this werewolf story?" he asked his brother later in their room.

"Don't know," Joe replied, pulling off his T-shirt. "Funny coincidence, that glowing wolf-dog turning up at the diner. But I think it's just as wise we didn't mention it to Alena, or to Aunt Gertrude or Mother, for that matter."

"Check," Frank agreed.

Some time later, the boys awoke with a start from the sound of a gunshot. It was followed instantly by a heavy thud at the front of their house!

2

A Silver Clue

Frank and Joe were out of bed in a jiffy, hastily flinging on clothes.

"Where'd that loud thump come from?" Joe asked excitedly, tugging on his jeans.

"Our front door, I think!" Frank replied.

They were met in the hallway by their mother and Aunt Gertrude, both in night robes, their aunt with her hair pinned up in curlers.

"One of you call the police, please!" Frank suggested as he and Joe hurried downstairs.

"What about you two?" Mrs. Hardy asked as the women followed anxiously.

"Don't be foolish!" Gertrude Hardy scolded her nephews. "If you go out the front door, you may be making targets of yourselves."

"Smart thinking, Aunty," Joe agreed. "We'll use a window instead."

He and Frank squirmed out a side window in case either the front or back door was being covered by the unknown enemy. Splitting up, they searched the grounds cautiously, only to meet again ten minutes later. Neither had sighted any intruder.

Just then they heard the front door open, and their aunt, who had been watching them through the window, called out, "The phone's dead!"

"No wonder, the line's been cut," Joe reported after picking out the dangling wire with his flashlight.

"I'll go find a police car or a public phone booth," Frank said. "You stay with Mom and Aunt Gertrude, Joe."

He quickly backed their car out of the garage and headed for the nearest storefront street. After beaming out a call over the police waveband, he soon sighted a responding prowl car and guided the officers to the Hardy house.

When they arrived, Joe was busy with a knife at the front door. "You were right, Frank," he reported. "Look what I dug out of the wood!" He held up a small, gleaming lump of metal.

"That looks like silver," exclaimed one of the policemen. He stared at the Hardys. "You mean this was fired into your front door?"

Frank nodded.

"Seems as if you have a new enemy," the other officer added.

13

Frank shrugged. "Or an old one. Who knows?"

The two patrolmen promised to cruise around the area, keeping a sharp lookout for suspicious characters. Later they would take the bullet to the police lab for ballistic examination.

As they drove off, Joe glanced at his brother. "A silver bullet! You know what that means?"

"You bet I do! According to superstition, that's the only kind that will kill a werewolf!"

"Boy, I wouldn't believe this if I heard it on the news," said Joe. "Do you suppose it means someone in town really thinks a werewolf is haunting Bayport?"

"Could be," Frank mused. "It could also mean that someone's warning us not to meddle in the Tabor case."

Even though the next day was Sunday, the telephone company sent out a special repairman to reconnect the Hardys' line. Meanwhile, Frank and Joe went to church with their mother and aunt. Afterwards they drove to the Morton farm, where they found Chet building a birchbark canoe.

The stout youth was stripped to the waist and perspiring freely in the hot August sunshine. He struggled to shape a huge strip of bark to a framework of cedar ribs and gunwales fitted around maple thwarts.

"Hey, not bad," Joe said admiringly.

"Except for one thing," Frank pointed out.

Chet shot him a peevish glance. "What's that?"

"You're supposed to shape the skin first and fit the ribs inside it. At least that was the Indian way."

14

"Listen! I know what I'm doing," said Chet, puffing and grunting.

"You'd better." Joe grinned. "You might just have to demonstrate that thing to us on a chilly mountain river before long."

"What do you mean?"

"We're going to a cottage in the Adirondacks for a week or two and you're invited to tag along," Frank replied. "Want to come?"

A dazzling smile burst over Chet's chubby face. "Wow! Do I!" he exclaimed, releasing his pressure on the birchbark.

Next moment he toppled over backwards as the tough, curling bark flapped back, knocking him galley-west. Roaring with laughter at Chet's surprised look, Frank and Joe helped him wrestle the birchbark back in place and secure it temporarily with clamps.

"I've been soaking that stuff since breakfast," their roly-poly pal complained, "but it dries out faster than I get it on."

Chet's usual good humor soon returned as he thought about their upcoming trip to the Adirondacks. "How soon do we leave?" he asked.

"Tomorrow morning," Frank responded. "Can you be ready by then?"

"You bet! This'll really give me a chance to show you how those old mountain men used to live out in the wilderness!"

"I can hardly wait." Joe chuckled.

"Don't worry, you'll see," Chet boasted. "Which reminds me. I've got something that belongs to one of you."

He trotted off to the front porch of the Morton farmhouse and returned with a lightweight jacket, which he tossed to Frank.

"That's the one I left at the diner last night," Frank said. "How'd you find it?"

"I didn't," Chet replied. "Someone else did."

"Who was it?"

"Search me. He never mentioned his name. I tried to call you last night but couldn't get through."

"Someone cut our phone line," Joe explained.

"No kidding!" Chet said that he had received a late call from a man who supposedly also failed to reach the Hardys by telephone. "The guy spotted your name tag in the jacket, Frank. When he couldn't get you, Nick Pappadopolos remembered seeing us all at the diner together and suggested he call me."

"What happened then?" Frank asked.

"I told him I knew you, so he said he'd drop off the jacket."

"Mighty nice of him," Joe remarked.

"Sure was. And this must belong to him," said Frank, picking up a key which had fallen out of a pocket when Chet tossed the jacket to him.

"How come?" his stout chum asked.

"It's not mine, and I'm sure it wasn't in my pocket last night."

16

"He must've stuck it in there absentmindedly," said Joe. "Tough break. He may be looking all over for that key. We ought to give it back to him. What'd the guy look like, Chet?"

"I don't know. He never rang our bell, so I didn't meet him. Probably came by late and didn't want to disturb us. I found the jacket lying on the porch this morning."

Frank, wanting to return the favor, decided to drive to the diner and see if Nick Pappadopolos knew the man who had found his jacket. To the Hardys' surprise, Nick had no idea what Frank was talking about.

"Nobody was in here last night asking about you," the proprietor declared, "and I never told anyone Chet Morton was a buddy of yours."

Frank and Joe looked at each other with puzzled frowns.

"Oh, Nick, sorry we bothered you," Frank said. Then the Hardys returned to the parking lot and climbed in their car.

"How do you figure it, Frank?" Joe asked. "Do you suppose Chet got the story wrong?"

Frank shook his head. "I doubt it. But there's something fishy somewhere."

"Like the way your jacket turned up on Chet's front porch, for instance."

The older Hardy boy nodded. "Maybe the guy didn't want to be seen."

"Let's have another look at that key, Frank." Joe took

17

it from his brother and examined it. The key was small and flat, with one serrated edge, and was stamped with the number 27.

"Looks like the kind that might open an airport locker," Joe suggested.

"Yes, except that airports don't usually have rental lockers anymore," Frank pointed out. "Too easy for terrorists to stash bombs in them."

"Wait a minute! The Bayport bus station still has lockers!"

"Right. Want to check them out?"

"Why not?"

On their way, Frank braked for a traffic light and pulled alongside a pickup truck belonging to the Prito Construction Company. Their pal, Tony Prito, was at the wheel with Biff Hooper beside him.

"What's up?" the muscular, dark-haired youth inquired through the open window.

The Hardys told them about their trip to the Adirondacks and invited their friends to come along.

"Boy, I wish I could," Tony said wistfully. "But Dad's keeping me too busy."

"Same here," said Biff. "I've been working at that construction site on Ridge Road."

"If the job gets done fast enough, we could come up for a day or two later on," Tony added.

"What's cooking with you Hardys?" Biff asked. "Another mystery?"

"Sort of, but just a small one right now." Frank

showed them the key and related the odd way in which his jacket had turned up on the Mortons' front porch after the stranger's call to Chet.

"But why would the guy give Chet a phony story?" Biff inquired.

"That's what we'd like to know," Joe replied. "If we can get a lead on who he is, maybe we can find out."

Tony and Biff were in no hurry. They had been checking the Ridge Road construction site to make sure no vandalism was taking place over the weekend. So they decided to accompany the Hardys to the bus station.

Joe's hunch was borne out when the key proved to fit locker number 27. Frank opened the door. A wrapped package lay inside.

"Any name or address on it?" Joe asked eagerly.

"Let's see." Frank lifted out the package to examine it. Suddenly he held it toward his ear as if to listen. "It's ticking!" he announced tensely.

"Leaping lizards!" Joe gasped. "It must be a bomb!"

3

Weird Lore

The youths stared at each other with stunned expressions. The package in Frank's hands might be laden with death and destruction!

"Better call the police!" Tony croaked.

"No time," said Frank. "When I moved this out of the locker, I may have armed the detonator and started the ticking." He glanced frantically at the Sunday travelers milling about the station.

"At least get it outside!" urged Joe.

"Right!" said Frank, who was already hurrying toward the entrance. "The problem is where to dump it!"

As the four dashed out to the street, Tony had an idea. "There's an old brick warehouse in the next block that's ready for the wrecker's ball!" he suggested.

"Just the place!" Frank agreed.

The boys ran desperately toward the warehouse, aware that with every passing second the package in Frank's hands might be ticking closer to disaster. As they reached the building, Frank gave a mighty heave and hurled the package into the fenced-off loading dock area.

Ka-booom! It hit the ground and exploded in a cloud of smoke and small flying debris. The blast was loud, but the concussion was not great. When the smoke cleared, there was no visible sign of damage to the building. Passersby paused in alarm and looked at the boys suspiciously, then hurried on about their business.

All four youths were pale and perspiring, but their faces now wore relieved smiles.

"Wow!" said Biff in a small voice. "The jolt when it hit the ground must have set off the bomb!"

"Thank goodness it was just a small one," Tony declared.

"It still wouldn't have done Frank any good if he'd been holding it," Joe pointed out. "Or the rest of us, either."

The next morning Frank and Joe stopped at the Morton farmhouse to pick up Chet. When they got underway again half an hour later, the car was loaded down with luggage and assorted gear, including their pal's handcrafted bow and a quiverful of arrows. In addition, his unfinished canoe was strapped to the car roof.

21

"For crying out loud, Chet," Joe complained, "we're only going to a cottage for a week, not on a full-scale wilderness expedition!"

"Listen, when you head into rugged country like the Adirondacks, you have to be ready for anything," retorted their stout chum, who was wedged into the car's narrow back seat. "I aim to be prepared!"

Their route from the Morton farm led back through Bayport. On the way, Joe suggested stopping at the library to see if they could find a book dealing with the subject of werewolves.

"What do you want that for?" Chet asked curiously.

"That's why we're going up to the Adirondacks. To hunt down a werewolf!" Joe explained.

"A *werewolf!*" Chet exclaimed, bug-eyed. "Are you serious?"

"Sure, it's a new case we're on," said Joe. "Didn't we mention that?"

"No, you didn't! If I'd known you were going to be tangling with some bloodthirsty wolfman nut, I'd have thought twice about coming!"

"What's to be scared of?" Frank teased. "If you run into him, the worst he can do is sink his fangs into your throat."

"Very funny," Chet said sourly. "Har-de-har-har with the Hardy boys."

"That's the spirit." Frank chuckled. "If the werewolf gets you, at least you'll die laughing!"

At the library, the Hardys consulted Miss Shannon at

the reference desk. She went straight to a bookshelf of new editions and brought back a volume with a colorful wrapper.

"This may be just what you're looking for," she advised. "It's a recent best-seller by a writer named Desmond Quorn. He's compiled all sorts of folklore and superstitions about werewolves, and he describes a number of alleged cases from old records."

"Sounds perfect," Frank said. "Thanks a lot."

After checking out the book, the Hardys rejoined their roly-poly chum, who was waiting sulkily in the car.

"Cheer up, Chet," said Joe. "Just one more stop."

"Now where?"

"Police headquarters."

"Oh, no!" Chet groaned. "Don't tell me there's even more trouble ahead, besides werewolves?"

"Nothing serious," Joe replied, suppressing a grin. "Just want to see about a bullet I dug out of our front door Saturday night."

"I knew it! That means there's a gunman after you guys, probably some mobster on the FBI's Most Wanted List!"

"Why do you suppose we brought *you* along?" Joe said with a straight face. "If there's a car chase and the bullets start flying, we'll have a shield of blubber protecting us in the back seat!"

Even Frank could not help laughing as he saw Chet's expression in the rearview mirror. But despite Joe's teasing, both Hardys knew there was no better friend in a tight spot than Chet Morton.

At headquarters they spoke to Chief Collig, a long-time acquaintance of their father's. He had a technician bring the bullet to his office from the ballistics lab.

"What can you tell us?" Frank inquired.

"It's definitely silver," the lab officer said. "Hand cast in a mold, I imagine."

"Enough marks to identify the gun?"

"No way. It's too mashed up. But my guess, judging from the weight of the slug, would be that it was fired from a .22."

"Probably some nut heard about the spooky dog you fellows sighted at the diner the other night," Chief Collig suggested. "So he got the wild notion there was a werewolf haunting Bayport and figured he might scare it off with a silver bullet."

"Could be," Frank murmured doubtfully.

"Anyhow, we'll keep an eye out for any local mental cases or oddballs on the loose with a gun," the chief promised.

"Thanks. By the way, Joe and I are going away for a few days. If you could have the scout car in our neighborhood check our house now and again at night, we'd appreciate it."

"Will do!"

The Hardys drove out of town and by eleven o'clock were on the New York State Thruway, heading north to the Adirondacks.

24

"My stomach's hollow," Chet complained. "Couldn't we stop for a bite to eat?"

"Too early for lunch," Joe objected.

"I don't mean a full meal. Just a quick snack to keep going, like a couple of burgers and fries."

"Okay." Frank grinned, veering off the road toward a diner. "This place looks decent."

Joe took the library book on werewolves inside and looked at it while they were in a booth waiting to be served. A picture of the author, Desmond Quorn, was on the back flap of the jacket.

"It says he lives near Kingston, New York," Joe remarked. "We'll be going right by there!"

"Hm, that's a thought," Frank agreed. "He might be able to give us some useful information."

The Hardys decided to call the author from the phone booth in the diner. Frank soon found his number by dialing information. Quorn immediately recognized the Hardys by name and invited them and their friend to have lunch with him.

"Thanks, we'll be happy to, sir," Frank said.

He and Joe had nothing but root beer and let Chet polish off the hamburgers they had ordered. But by the time they reached Kingston, Chet assured them that the snack had in no way spoiled his appetite for lunch.

The author's home proved to be a lovely old Dutch Colonial farmhouse. Desmond Quorn himself was a tall, thin man with graying blond hair and horn-rimmed glasses. An interesting talker with a fund of occult lore,

25

he fascinated the boys throughout lunch with yarns and legends about vampires and werewolves.

"What's your opinion, Mr. Quorn?" Chet asked uneasily between mouthfuls of apple pie. "Are there really such things as werewolves?"

Quorn shrugged and smiled. "I neither believe nor disbelieve. It just happens to be my hobby to collect all the folklore on the subject. But werewolves have certainly been reported in many countries, and a lot of people did believe in them in olden days."

"There's a scientific word for the belief that people can turn into wolves, isn't there?" said Frank.

"Yes, the word is *lycanthropy*. There's also a disease called *porphyria*, which may lead to mental disturbance. It can cause hair to grow on the skin and even make a person so sensitive to light that he prefers to stay in the dark and go out only at night. Possibly some so-called werewolf cases were just people suffering from *porphyria*."

"Where do you dig up reports on werewolf cases?"

"In old records of European court trials, to name one source," the author explained. "You see, in the Middle Ages, werewolves were supposed to be possessed by the Devil, or to have made a pact with him. The judges who condemned people to be burned at the stake as witches sometimes had so-called werewolves put to death, too. The name werewolf, by the way, comes from Anglo-Saxon words meaning 'man-wolf'."

Desmond Quorn added that there are also a number

of old books and writings on the subject, besides the stories handed down from one generation to another. He said he had many cases in his files, collected from all these sources.

"Would you by any chance have a record of a Bohemian werewolf named Tabor?" Joe asked as they all rose from the lunch table.

Quorn flashed him a curious glance. "Of course. And how odd you should ask. It so happens that twice recently I've had occasion to look up that case."

He led the boys into his study and pulled out a file drawer. The next moment he turned around with a startled expression on his face.

"What's wrong, sir?" Frank asked.

"My data on the Tabor case!" Quorn exclaimed. "It's been stolen!"

4

Telltale Limp

The Hardys were as startled as their host. They could not help wondering if the theft had anything to do with their own investigation.

"What makes you so sure the information was stolen?" Frank asked.

"Because the papers were right here in this folder last Friday," Quorn replied. "And I haven't consulted the file since then!"

"Any idea who might have taken them?"

"Indeed I do," the author replied angrily. "I had a visitor on Friday named Julien Sorel, who also inquired about the Tabor case. He must have snitched the records from the file folder when I left the room for a few moments."

"Know anything about him?"

"Nothing, except that he spoke with a French accent. He phoned and said he had read and enjoyed my book, and asked if he could stop in to get my autograph. Then when he was here, he brought up the Tabor case."

Frank said, "Did he mention where he was from?"

Quorn hesitated. "No, but from things he said, I got the impression that he had just arrived in this country recently, perhaps as a tourist."

Their host soon recovered from his annoyance and was able to tell the Hardys the main facts of the case in question, since he had checked and discussed it only a few days earlier.

"According to legend, the Tabors bore a curse," he related. "The family was said to spawn a werewolf every seventh generation, which was roughly every two hundred years. The last case occurred in the eighteenth century, somewhere around 1760. But there are records of two previous ancestors being condemned as werewolves in the fourteenth and sixteenth centuries."

"What happened to the last one?" Joe asked.

"His name was Jan Tabor. The story goes that he was shot in the leg by a huntsman with a silver bullet one night while he was prowling about in the form of a wolf. The next morning he turned into a human again, but the huntsman spotted him because he was limping from the bullet. So his vengeful neighbors dragged him off to the town square to be tried as a werewolf."

"Wow!" Chet shuddered. "That kind of stuff gives me the creeps!"

"In those days," Quorn continued, "it was dangerous to be thought different from other people, or to get your neighbors mad at you."

"You mentioned there were two times recently when you had occasion to look up your files on the Tabors," Frank said.

Desmond Quorn nodded. "Yes, another reader called three or four months ago to inquire about them, when my book first came out. I don't think he gave me any name, or if he did, I don't remember."

After thanking their host for the pleasant lunch, the Hardys and Chet continued their journey. All three were thrilled by the magnificent scenery of the Adirondack region, a land of rugged mountains, swift rivers, sweet-smelling deep green forests and still blue lakes.

They telephoned Alena Tabor before reaching Hawk River and found her waiting for them when they arrived later that afternoon. The cottage, built of hewn logs, stood on a bank of the river. Alena came out to greet them as they pulled up in front.

"I'm so glad you could make it," she said after the Hardys had introduced Chet. "You're just in time for a party!"

"Sounds great." Joe grinned. "What sort of party?"

"A barbecue at our house. It starts at seven o'clock this evening." She gave the boys directions for getting there and added, "You'll have a chance to meet my father and brother, too."

"You said your brother's name was John, didn't you?" Frank asked.

"That's right."

"Which would be the same as the Czech name, Jan, wouldn't it?"

Alena nodded, her expression immediately turning serious. "Yes, and by a strange coincidence, that was the name of the last alleged werewolf in the Tabor family. Jan Tabor was the father of the Hessian mercenary who came to America."

She told the boys that her mother had died several years ago, and that the woman who now kept house for the Tabors was half Mohawk Indian.

"We call her Pocahontas, or just Pokey." Alena smiled. "She looks a bit stern and overpowering, but don't let her bulldoze you when you meet her. Incidentally, I'll introduce you as chums of my girlfriend in Oakville. You can pretend you're renting the cottage. That way, neither my brother nor anyone else will be suspicious of you."

"Suits us," Joe said.

The cottage was comfortably furnished with dishes and bedding, and even had a telephone. But Chet paid no attention to any of it. Instead, he looked out the window as Alena drove off in her car.

"Wow! What a knockout!" he murmured. Judging by the bashful admiration he had bestowed on her when introduced, it was apparent to the Hardys that Chet had fallen hard for the rosy-cheeked girl.

"It's her plumpness he likes," Joe whispered loudly behind his hand to Frank.

"What do you mean, plumpness?" Chet retorted. "Her dimensions are perfect!"

A red sunset was blazing behind the tall pine trees and an appetizing smell of steak was wafting from the barbecue pit when the three Bayporters arrived at the Tabor home. It was a handsome house of gray fieldstone that seemed to fit perfectly in its wilderness setting. Adjoining the house was a patio and enclosed swimming pool on one side, and a hangar for Karel Tabor's private helicopter on the other.

"What a beautiful home you have!" Frank told Alena after she had shown them around.

"My father designed it himself," she said proudly.

Mr. Tabor was a broad-shouldered man of about fifty. The boys could see that his daughter took after him in features, but unlike her, he looked rather pale and gaunt. At the moment, he was welcoming guests and keeping an eye on the sizzling beef, but as soon as everyone was served, he made it a point to draw up a camp chair near the Hardys, Alena, and Chet.

"Your father came to my office in New York not long ago, in connection with an insurance investigation," Karel Tabor told Frank and Joe, "and from all I hear, you two seem to have inherited his knack for detection."

32

"We've learned a lot from watching Dad and working with him," said Frank.

"Well, I certainly hope you can shed some light on this mystery that's—," the architect broke off and his expression changed to a somewhat forced smile as a slender, wiry-looking young man in a plaid flannel shirt and jeans approached. "This is my son, John," Mr. Tabor said to the Hardys and Chet.

John had the same curly brown hair and features as his father and sister, but also a tense, nervous manner. He barely seemed to register the boys' names as they were introduced and shook hands.

"You fellows must be new in these parts," he said, obviously trying to make polite conversation.

"They're friends of Magda's down in Oakville," Alena put in hastily. "They're renting our river cottage for a week or so."

"Hope you enjoy yourselves," John commented, his glance roving over the other guests and the flickering flames from the barbecue pit.

Alena urged her brother to try some of the steak and barbecue sauce. But he shrugged her suggestion aside, saying he was not hungry, and soon excused himself to wander off restlessly.

Mr. Tabor sighed and shook his head. "I wish we knew what was troubling him," he murmured as soon as John was out of earshot.

"Alena tells us he's an architect, too," Frank remarked.

The elder Tabor nodded. "Yes, and a highly gifted one, if I do say so. At any rate, he's done some apprentice work for our company during his last two years of study, and it certainly shows great promise, not to mention the prizes he's won."

"What's the name of your firm?" Joe asked.

"Chelsea Builders. It's actually a corporation with stockholders and a board of directors. I'm just the president. I didn't mean to imply that I own the firm."

"How did your son's trouble start?" said Frank.

"When he was studying for his licensing exam," Mr. Tabor replied, "he worked too hard. I'm afraid that brought on his breakdown. After a while he began to show signs of nervous exhaustion. That's when he began harking back to this old family legend about werewolves. So I persuaded him to go to a mental sanatorium for treatment, the Pine Manor Rest Home in the Catskills."

"Did that help?"

Mr. Tabor shook his head. "Frankly, no. He left the sanatorium on his own accord, and I made no objection since he showed no sign of improvement. In fact, in some ways he seemed worse. By then the fear seemed to be preying on him that he himself might be turning into a werewolf. I thought it might be better to keep his mind occupied, so I agreed that he should come home and resume his studies."

"How about the local werewolf scare, around Hawk River?" Joe put in. "When did all that start?"

"About the same time John returned. And to make matters worse, he's developed a habit of slipping out of the house at night during the full moon—at least he did during the last full-moon period. Then, when he shows up again, he can't remember where he's been or what he's been doing."

As if by common impulse, both Hardys found their glances straying upward. Darkness had fallen, and the moon shone in the black-blue sky like a round copper coin.

"I know what you're thinking, and that's exactly what I'm afraid of too—that John may start acting strangely again," Mr. Tabor said gloomily. "But I'm also afraid of saying anything or mentioning these local werewolf stories for fear of upsetting him or maybe making his delusions worse."

"But why should John expect the curse to fall on *him*?" Frank inquired. "There must be lots of other members of the Tabor family still in Europe."

"No, actually there aren't," said the architect. "The last alleged werewolf, Jan Tabor, had only one other son besides my ancestor who came to this country. Most of his descendants in the old country were wiped out during World War II. So far as I know, our only relative who still bears the family name is a distant cousin. He escaped from behind the Iron Curtain just before Czechoslovakia fell under Communist rule after the war."

The conversation seemed to have left Mr. Tabor

looking rather haggard and depressed. He plucked a bottle of pills from his pocket and excused himself to get a glass of water.

"Dad has a weak heart," Alena explained to the boys in a low, concerned voice. "This worry about John is an added strain on him."

She looked up nervously as a series of weird, comical howls split the darkness.

Arrooo-o-o—Arrooo-o-o!

"What on earth was that?" Alena exclaimed.

A figure wearing a rubber Halloween wolfman mask over his head emerged from among the trees into the circle of firelight and the glow of the patio lamps. He hobbled rapidly across the lawn and disappeared into the woods on the other side of the house.

The weird-looking intruder touched off a wave of nervous laughter among the guests, while Frank and Joe darted off in pursuit.

"Which way did he go? Can you see him?" Joe called out to his brother as they probed about in the darkness.

"Nope, not a glimpse. We should've brought flashlights. I guess we're out of luck."

As the Hardys returned to the barbecue party, Chet came to meet them, looking surprised. "What did you two get so excited about? That goofy wolfman act was just a joke."

"Like fun it was," Frank retorted. "That was an intentional dirty trick, and whoever pulled it knew all about the Tabor werewolf legend."

5

A Frightening Phantom

"What do you mean?" Chet asked with a puzzled frown.

"Didn't you notice the way the guy was limping?" said Frank.

"Not only that, he had a big reddish stain on his trouser leg," Joe put in, "as if he might have been bleeding from a gunshot wound, just like the last accused werewolf, Jan Tabor, in the 1700s!"

Chet stared at the Hardys uneasily for a moment. Then he flashed a nervous grin and tried to scoff the matter aside. "Aw, don't tell me you take that stuff seriously?"

"Of course not," Frank said. "Jan Tabor was probably just an innocent victim of hysteria, same as those

37

poor women who were condemned in the Salem witchcraft trials in colonial days. The point is, Alena told us no one around here knew about that old legend and their family curse. But that wise guy in the wolf-man mask sure did, and he was deliberately trying to upset the Tabors!"

The boys glanced at Alena and her father, who were both shaken by the unpleasant prank.

"Where's John?" muttered Joe.

"Over there," Chet said, pointing discreetly to the refreshment table. From the expression on young Tabor's face, he seemed more nervous and keyed-up than ever.

Frank and Joe could overhear other guests nearby chattering about what had happened.

"I wish I could believe that thing that was prowling around Hawk River last month was just some joker in a rubber mask!" said one voice.

"Whatever it was that scared our dog and broke into the Barnett's henhouse had more than rubber fangs!" said another.

"And just think, it may show up again tonight! There's another full moon out!"

"How soon do you start back to school?" Joe asked Alena loudly to distract her from paying any attention to the remarks.

"Right after Labor Day," she replied.

"What school do you attend?" Chet inquired.

"A boarding school in eastern New York."

"Hi you! John!" shouted a bellowing but evidently female voice suddenly. "Phone call!"

The boys were startled, as much by the sight of the speaker as by the sheer booming volume of her voice. She was a huge woman, with black braids hanging down on each side of her coppery-skinned face, and was clad in a shapeless brown sweater pulled over a bright red-and-yellow gingham housedress.

"That's Pocahontas." Alena giggled, seeing the Hardys' and Chet's stunned expressions. "She's our cook and housekeeper, not to say general boss lady of the establishment; at least she would be if we gave her half a chance!"

John Tabor followed her meekly into the house. When he came out again a few minutes later, Frank and Joe noticed that he seemed strangely silent and withdrawn. He did not even reply when one of the guests spoke to him.

The party broke up around ten o'clock.

"Did you see how John was acting after he got that phone call?" Frank remarked to his brother as the boys drove back to the cottage.

"I'll say I did! He was walking around like a zombie."

Chet was ready to change into pajamas and flop down on his bunk, to recuperate from their exhausting trip from Bayport, followed by the open-air barbecue.

But Joe stopped him. "Hey! Where do you think you're going?"

"To bed, where else?"

39

"Guess again, pal. Our evening hasn't even started yet."

Chet stared in heavy-lidded, open-mouthed dismay. "What do you mean, it hasn't even started? I'm ready to hit the hay. Aren't you?"

"Tell him, Frank."

The older Hardy slapped Chet on the shoulder. "We could use some shut-eye, all right. But we've got other plans and we need your help."

"How?"

"You saw that full moon," Frank replied. "Which means the werewolf could be out again tonight. Joe and I'll scout around the village, but we'd like you to keep watch outside the Tabors' house. If John doesn't come out, but the werewolf still appears, it proves John isn't the nut who's terrorizing Hawk River."

Chet's face fell, but with his usual good nature and stout-hearted gumption he agreed to the Hardys' plan.

Just then a weird, wailing sound was heard.

Chet gulped. "What was that?"

The sound came again faintly.

"Seemed like a wolf howl!" exclaimed Joe.

He and Frank dashed out of the cabin, followed less enthusiastically by Chet, but the boys could see nothing in the moonlit darkness. Nor was the sound repeated.

"Maybe it was just the wind," Frank concluded.

Shortly before eleven o'clock, the boys put on warm lumberjackets and climbed into the Hardys' car. With Joe at the wheel, they took the river road and headed toward the Tabor estate.

40

Parking their car in a grove of trees some distance from the drive, they approached the house on foot. The windows were not yet dark, and from time to time they could glimpse moving figures inside, one of whom was recognizable as John Tabor.

"Good. So we know he's home," Frank murmured.

One by one the lights went out, and presently the whole household seemed to be wrapped in slumbering darkness.

"Okay, get settled, you brawny North Woodsman!" Joe said to Chet.

The Hardys lent their shoulders and hands to their stout chum to help him clamber up into the crotch of a tree, where he managed to prop himself firmly against the trunk. From this point he had a full view of the house.

"If John Tabor sticks his nose out, you follow him," Frank instructed Chet.

"Right. Leave him to me, fellows! If he thinks he's going to flash his fangs around Hawk River tonight without being spotted, he has another thing coming!"

Waving good-by to their friend, the Hardys started out toward the village on foot, leaving their car where it was. A breeze had sprung up, bringing a chilly hint of the crisp fall weather to come. The boys were glad they had their lumberjackets and caps as they trudged along. The mountain scenery loomed all around them, looking more magnificent than ever in the daylight.

The village of Hawk River consisted of one main business street, which ran parallel to the water, with

several side streets and unpaved dirt lanes crossing it. Beyond them the houses straggled off toward outlying farms and orchards.

Frank and Joe roved about quietly, seeing no one. They had brought flashlights, but had little need of them due to the bright full moon. Soon they heard the town-hall clock chime midnight.

"The witching hour!" Joe chuckled.

They reached the end of one of the side streets and decided to continue into more open country. Minutes later both boys stiffened as a distant howl echoed through the night, then another!

"Come on!" cried Frank. "That must be the real thing!"

They ran in the direction of the sounds and presently saw a figure dashing toward them out of the darkness. It proved to be a boy their own age, obviously scared out of his wits!

"What's the matter?" Frank called out as the youth came closer.

"I just saw a wolf back there!" the boy panted. "It came right at me, and the thing glowed in the dark!"

6

The Missing Suspect

Having seen such a beast themselves, the Hardys were not inclined to laugh at the youth's fantastic story. He was so terrified that he would have kept on running had they not each taken him by an arm and calmed him.

"Look, no werewolf's going to get you," Joe assured him. "Not if we stick together. Whatever the thing is, it'll think twice before tackling all of us!"

To back up his promise, he broke off some thick branches from a windfallen tree nearby. Keeping one as a club to protect himself, he passed out the other two to his brother and the frightened teenager, who said his name was Bob Renaud.

When no wolf creature appeared, Bob plucked up his courage and accompanied the Hardys in search of

44

the glowing phantom. But the boys found no sign of the beast.

"It must have gone that way," Bob surmised, pointing to a fork in the road. "I dodged through the trees when I got this far, trying to shake it off, so it may have missed my trail."

"Tell us how you first sighted it," Frank asked.

"Well, I was out on a date with my girlfriend. I dropped her off at her house just after eleven-thirty and started driving home, when all of a sudden *bang!* I got a flat tire." Bob related that after pulling off the road, he had gotten out and jacked up the car in order to change the wheel.

"Then I heard a bloodcurdling wolf howl," he went on. "I looked around and saw this snarling thing coming at me, all glowing like a ghost! Boy, I'm telling you, I dropped everything and took off!" Bob shook his head, still a bit jittery at the recollection. "I hope you don't think I'm making all this up."

"Don't worry, we believe you," Frank assured him.

He and Joe escorted Bob to his car. By now, the boy had recovered his nerve, and he finished changing his tire. Then he waved good-by to the Hardys, who hurried back in the direction Bob had indicated.

"By now that critter could be a mile away," Joe mumbled.

"Maybe so, but let's keep looking," Frank urged. "It might howl again and give us an idea which way it's gone."

The words were barely out of his mouth when the breezy nighttime silence was shattered by an echoing shotgun blast. It was immediately followed by another as the unseen gunner let go his second barrel!

A startled look flashed between the Hardys. Without a word, they speeded up their pace, sprinting around a bend in the road just ahead.

A farmhouse loomed in the moonlight not far away. As Frank and Joe approached it, an angry-looking farmer burst out of the driveway gate, clutching a shotgun in one hand. He wore an old coat flung over a pair of long underwear, and rubber boots. Evidently he had pulled on the first thing that came to hand before charging out of his house.

"What happened?" Frank called out.

"That doggone werewolf!" the farmer fumed. "I heard it attacking my livestock in the barn, so I grabbed my gun and went after it!"

"You actually saw the creature?"

"You bet I did! It musta heard me comin'! Went boundin' outa the barn just as I ran through the back door toward the yard. I gave it both barrels, but the thing got away!"

"What did it look like?" Joe asked.

"Big wolf-dog! And its fur glowed fiery white. I'm not jokin', boys!"

Frank nodded. "We believe you. We just met another guy who saw it before it came here!"

"Which way did it go?" put in the younger Hardy.

"It leaped clear over this gate and went into them woods." The farmer pointed across the road.

Frank and Joe accompanied him as he probed about among the trees, lending their flashlights to the search. But the ghostly beast had disappeared. They finally said good night to the farmer and headed back to town.

A number of people in Hawk River had been wakened by the distant wolf howls. None of them, however, had glimpsed the prowling creature itself.

"I've a hunch that farmer was the last one to see it tonight," Frank remarked to his brother.

"Same here," Joe agreed. "Let's go and find out what Chet has to report."

As they approached the driveway of the Tabor estate, their ears were assailed by a strange, grating noise.

"Are you thinking what I'm thinking?" Joe asked.

"I'm afraid so," Frank replied. "But let's hope we're wrong."

Unfortunately they were not. The sound they had heard proved to be low, rumbling snores. Chet was slumped sound asleep in his snug tree perch, with his chin on his chest.

"Wake up, Strongheart!" said Joe, reaching up to tug the stout boy's ankle.

Chet twitched nervously and awoke with a violent start that almost sent him tumbling out of the tree into the arms of the Hardy boys.

"Wh-what happened?" he stuttered, clutching at the branch for support.

47

"Don't panic, the battle's over." Frank grinned. He and Joe related the night's sensational events.

"I don't suppose you'd know whether John Tabor sneaked out of the house?" Joe inquired.

"We-e-ell, actually no, I don't," Chet confessed shamefacedly. "But I sure didn't see any sign of him before I dozed off."

"Which was probably seconds after we left," said Frank. "I think we'd better wake up the Tabors."

Chet swung himself out of the tree and accompanied his pals up to the front door of the house. Frank decided not to ring the bell, hoping a knock or two might be less alarming.

Soon Karel Tabor himself appeared at the door. "Come in, boys," he said. "Is anything wrong?"

"The werewolf's on the prowl again, Mr. Tabor," Frank explained. "I hope you won't misunderstand our reason for coming here, but it might be a good idea to check if John's home in bed."

"Good thinking," the architect nodded. "I'm glad you came. Assuming John is upstairs, sound asleep, you fellows will be able to bear witness that he has nothing to do with this werewolf scare!"

Despite his words, the boys could tell from Mr. Tabor's expression and voice that he was far from confident that this was the case. He invited the Hardys and Chet to sit down while he went up to look in his son's room.

When he returned a few moments later, the young detectives knew at a glance that the news was bad.

"John's bed hasn't been slept in," the architect announced in a husky voice.

"That still doesn't prove he's the werewolf," Frank said, hoping to provide some comfort. "Have you any idea where he might have gone?"

"None." Mr. Tabor shook his head gloomily, not trusting himself to say any more for fear his voice might tremble.

"In that case, I'd like to wait here with Joe and Chet till he shows up," Frank suggested. "If our presence in the house won't bother you?"

"Not at all! Do stay, by all means. I'll be glad of any help you can give us."

Mr. Tabor asked Pocahontas to make coffee, and she went off with a glowering expression, shaking her head and mumbling to herself in Mohawk.

Presently Alena came down in her robe and slippers, having heard her father and the boys chatting in low voices.

"Is something wrong?" she inquired anxiously. An alarming thought flashed through her mind. "Dad," she added, "Has anything happened to John?"

Karel Tabor took his daughter's hand into his own. "He seems to have gone off somewhere, my dear," he said, "and the so-called werewolf just paid another visit to Hawk River."

"Oh, no!" Alena's face showed her distresss. "Isn't there anything we can do?"

"Nothing, except wait for John to come home."

"We don't mean to intrude," Frank said uncomfort-

49

ably, "but we'd like to be on hand to question your brother when he does return."

"Of course, please stay!" Alena replied. "Dad and I appreciate having you here to help."

The atmosphere eased somewhat when Pocahontas brought in the coffee. The group chatted as well as they could under the circumstances, and the Hardys reported what had happened during their nocturnal expedition in and beyond the village.

As their vigil lengthened and time dragged by, everyone's spirits drooped. The boys found it hard to keep their eyes open. However, they snapped wide awake when, soon after three o'clock, footsteps were heard outside and the front door opened.

"It's John!" Alena cried in relief. She sprang up from her chair and hurled herself into her brother's arms.

If she expected an equally cordial response, she was doomed to disappointment. Instead of greeting his sister with a smiling remark, John merely stared at her, his face blank and expressionless. He did not return the embrace, either.

"Where on earth have you been, Son?" his father demanded.

"Where have I been?" John echoed. Dull-eyed, he raised one hand and scratched his head slowly. "Search me. I haven't the faintest idea. In fact, I don't even know where I am now."

7

Forest Castle

"John! Don't you recognize your own home?" Alena shook her brother impatiently. "Why did you go out tonight? Tell us where you've been!"

The young architect did not reply. He shrugged off her questions in silence and started toward the stairway leading up to the second floor. But Alena grabbed him by the arm.

"Dad, something's wrong with him!" she cried. "He's acting so weirdly. Oughtn't we call a doctor?"

Karel Tabor hesitated before replying. "No, I don't think so. Whatever's wrong with John, he'll probably sleep it off. Calling a doctor would only provoke scandal and gossip. Don't you think so, boys?"

"I'm afraid you're right." Frank nodded. "It might

even lead to accusations that your son was responsible for tonight's werewolf scare, if the news ever leaked out."

"John is awfully drowsy and heavy-lidded," Joe pointed out. He had risen from the sofa with his brother to examine young Tabor more closely. "I'll bet he'll drop off to sleep and tomorrow he won't even remember all this."

"Probably not," Frank agreed, opening John's eyelids more widely with his thumb and forefinger in order to check his pupils. "From what Dad's told us about such things, I don't think he's been drugged, but he looks as if he's in a trance!"

John stood limply now, staring off into the distance, utterly indifferent to, or not even aware of, what was going on around him.

The Hardys helped his father lead him upstairs and put him to bed.

Next morning at their cabin, Frank and Joe were awakened by a radio call. They had taken a special transceiver with them to ensure communications with Bayport and their father in case of an emergency. Now a red light was flashing on the set, and a repeated buzz was coming from the loudspeaker.

Joe leaped out of bed and switched on the mike and scrambler. The tuning dial had already been set to the agreed-on frequency.

"H-2 here. Come in please. Do you read me?"

"Loud and clear. F-H calling."

"Hi, Dad. What's up?"

Fenton Hardy replied that he had returned to Bayport the previous night, only to find the boys gone. "I was interested to hear about your werewolf case," he went on.

Joe filled him in quickly and added, "Mr. Tabor says he's met you at his company office."

"That's right," the famous detective replied. "I'm investigating a case for Federal Insurance Underwriters. It involves three buildings that were designed by Karel Tabor, with the actual construction work supervised by his firm, Chelsea Builders. All three have suffered recent disasters."

"Wow! That's pretty unusual, isn't it?"

"So the insurance underwriters think. They feel it stretches coincidences a bit far."

"Exactly what sort of disasters were they?"

"A fire, a gas explosion, and an apparent structural collapse."

"Hm, interesting." Joe frowned thoughtfully. "Still, all three occurrences *could* be due to accidents, couldn't they, Dad?"

"Maybe, or to poor design or sabotage, or even a plain old jinx. It's my job to find out."

"Any leads yet?"

"Nothing sufficient to act on. But while you fellows are up in the Adirondacks region, there's something you can do for me."

"Sure, Dad. Just name it."

Mr. Hardy explained that Karel Tabor was known to be working on two new projects at the moment. One was the design of a Manhattan skyscraper. The other was the restoration of an historic timbered mansion not far from Hawk River, dating back to Revolutionary days.

The private investigator gave the exact location and continued, "I'd like you and Frank to drive there and look around. See if you can spot any clues or signs of possible trouble. If anything's about to go wrong, the insurance company would like to know beforehand, not after it's too late."

"We'll check it out," Joe promised.

"Good," Mr. Hardy replied. "Incidentally, don't mention any of this to Karel Tabor."

"Understood, Dad. We won't say a word." The younger Hardy boy hesitated a moment before asking, "If there *is* anything crooked about those three building disasters, do you really think Mr. Tabor could be mixed up in it?"

"Too early to tell, Joe. At this moment I wouldn't even speculate as to why an architect or builder might want to damage his own work. But until we know more, I guess my answer would have to be yes. Tabor is under a certain amount of suspicion."

So far, the Hardys and Chet had tended to sympathize with Mr. Tabor's werewolf trouble and his son's seeming involvement in the weird mystery. The possibility that the architect might be implicated in anything unethical or criminal shocked all three boys.

54

As soon as breakfast was over, Frank and Joe started out in their car, leaving Chet behind to hold down the fort. After stopping for gas at Hawk River, they drove north on Route 30.

The old timbered mansion of which their father had spoken was perched on a steep, wooded hill overlooking Indian Lake. Hardhatted workmen were busy restoring it, while a number of tourists and local people stood by, watching idly.

Frank pulled off the road into a convenient parking spot. Then he and Joe got out and approached the work site.

"What a huge mansion up here in the wilderness!" Joe muttered.

"Sure is," Frank agreed. "Looks as if it's been mouldering away for a while, too. I bet they'll have quite a job restoring it."

The immense, weatherbeaten house was constructed of hand-hewn timbers, some of them visibly rotted. But the structure had obviously been built by an oldtime master craftsman.

As the boys clambered up the slope for a closer view, someone suddenly yelled in alarm. "Look out!" The Hardys turned just in time to see a long crane arm swinging overhead. A heavy balk of timber which it had been carrying was slipping out of its sling!

The next instant something struck them from behind, and both boys pitched headlong on the ground. A split second later the timber balk crashed to earth, almost on the very spot where they had been standing!

The Hardys picked themselves up breathlessly. When Joe saw what a narrow escape they had had, he let out a faint gasp.

The man who had pushed them out of the way, a tall young construction worker, was standing on the other side of the fallen timber. "You two all right?" he called.

"Yes, we're okay," said Frank, dusting himself off. "Thanks for the shove." The thought flashed through his mind that what happened might have been no accident. Perhaps one of the workmen had recognized them, or someone had found out beforehand that Fenton Hardy was sending them to the site. But Frank quickly discarded the idea of an attempt on their lives when he saw the crew's obvious concern over the matter and realized that the young workman had risked his own life to save them.

"Sorry if we got in the way," Frank apologized.

"Wasn't your fault," the man replied. "That crane sling was improperly secured. Besides, the crew should have roped off this area to keep spectators out of danger."

He signaled the crane arm back into position and helped his mates put the balk of timber into its sling again. Then, after the load had been secured, it was hoisted over to the house to replace one of the rotted structural beams.

Joe noticed the muscular young fellow's bronzed hawklike features and long dark hair, tucked up under his steel hardhat. "Are you an Indian?" he asked curiously.

"That's right." The workman grinned. "I'm Mohawk, and proud of it."

"You must be one of those 'high-steel Mohawks' we've read about," said Frank.

"Right again." The Indian explained that he and many of his fellow tribesmen had been employed on numerous construction jobs in the New York area. Experience had shown they were especially well fitted for work on skyscrapers and bridges because their superb natural sense of balance enabled them to keep their footing on high girders.

Thrusting out his hand, the Indian added, "My name's Eagle, by the way, Hank Eagle."

"I'm Frank Hardy," Frank said, returning the handshake. "And this is my brother Joe."

Hank Eagle's face took on a pleasantly surprised expression. "Hey, don't tell me you're those two detectives, the sons of Fenton Hardy?"

The boys nodded. "We are."

"Your father was at our company office not long ago, talking to my boss."

"You work for Chelsea Builders?" Joe asked.

"Sure do," said Hank. "Usually in New York City, but today I was sent out here to report on the progress of this job. Mr. Tabor knows this is my neck of the woods, and—well, I'm hoping to be an architect myself someday, if I can ever get my degree. But that takes a lot of night courses."

"Good for you," Frank said. "Stick with it."

"You fellows doing any detective work right now?" the Mohawk inquired, giving them a shrewd glance.

"Oh, in a way," Joe replied cautiously, remembering his father's admonition and trying to sound casual. "We were up here in the Adirondacks on vacation, and Dad's been investigating those disasters that happened to three other architectural projects of Mr. Tabor's, so he asked us to drop up to Indian Lake to look for any signs of trouble."

"Confidentially," Hank said, "that's why my boss sent *me* here, too. I'm sure glad to know I've got a couple of smart guys like you backing me up."

He offered to show the boys the interior of the mansion, and Frank and Joe gladly accepted. The huge building had a high balcony jutting out from the upper floor. Its original wooden supports had rotted away, so it had been propped up with temporary piling until they could be replaced. The balcony offered a breathtaking view of the green forested hillside and the vast, crystal-blue lake spread out below.

"Really beautiful!" Frank murmured, enjoying the scenery and inhaling the tangy mountain air. "Who ever built this place?"

"A British Indian agent, some time before the Revolutionary War," their Mohawk friend replied.

"Over two hundred years ago!" Joe exclaimed.

"Right." Hank nodded. "He was King George's personal envoy to the Indians in this part of America. He put up the mansion as his castle in the forest and got

58

very buddy-buddy with all the Iroquois nations, including the Mohawks. In fact, he married a Mohawk squaw, whose brother was—well, the Iroquois nations didn't really have chiefs, but her brother was one of their tribal leaders or wise men, only younger than most. His Mohawk name, translated into English, meant 'Dark Eagle,' and he was one of my ancestors," Hank said proudly.

"No kidding!" Frank was impressed.

"Yup, my great-great-great grandfather, or something like that."

"That means the British agent who was King George's personal rep was your great-great-great granduncle."

"Which may connect you to British nobility," Joe pointed out.

Hank Eagle burst out laughing. "You can't prove it by me, but in a way you're not so far off. You see, like most of the Iroquois, the Mohawks were close allies of the British, who had helped them fight the French. So when the American Revolution came along, they sided with their old pals, the Redcoats, against the Yankee settlers. And the British were anxious to keep it that way, so they invited Dark Eagle over to London and gave him the big hello. He actually met the King and hobnobbed with all the nobility at court. According to the history books, he was good-looking and his brother-in-law, the British agent, had had him well educated, so they made quite a fuss over him."

Frank said, "But he still helped the Redcoats against our side, I presume."

"Yup, he did," Hank admitted. "He even led some of the Tory-Indian scalping raids on the American settlements. But you have to remember, those were pretty bloody times."

After the war, Hank related, Dark Eagle made peace with his Yankee enemies and inherited his brother-in-law's timber castle, which he renamed Eagle's Nest. Years later, it lapsed into ruin. Now the wooden mansion had been purchased by a wealthy buyer, who had hired the architect Karel Tabor to restore it.

"Were you raised around here?" Joe asked as the boys walked outside again.

"Sure was, in a Mohawk village near Hawk River. You'll have to visit me there sometime. My uncle's the medicine man."

Frank noticed a man watching them closely. He was elderly and wizened-looking, with dark glasses and long gray hair. When he realized he had been noticed, the stranger turned suddenly and hurried away.

"Wait a minute!" Frank called and went after him. But before he could overtake the eavesdropper, his quarry leaped into a green foreign-made car and sped off!

8

A Sinking Feeling

The man gunned his engine hard. When he took off, his rear wheels churned up a cloud of dust, and the car's back end slewed around sharply as he swung onto the paved highway. As a result, Frank was not able to spot the license number.

Disgusted, the Hardy boy returned to his brother and their Mohawk friend, Hank Eagle.

"What happened?" Joe asked.

"That fellow was eavesdropping on us," Frank said angrily. "Did you get a look at him?"

"Yes," Joe replied. "Enough to recognize him again. He had on dark glasses—sort of an oldish guy, with long gray hair curling down over his ears."

"Right." Frank had noticed a strange look pass over

the Indian's face on hearing the man's description. "Do you know him, Hank?"

The Mohawk shrugged. "We get a lot of people stopping by to watch us. I may have seen him before. Hard to say."

Later, after thanking their newfound friend for his interesting guided tour of the work site, the Hardys drove back to Hawk River. "Did you notice the way Hank reacted when you described that eavesdropper?" Frank asked Joe.

"I sure did—as if he was covering up something." Joe added wryly, "Something tells me he was attempting to be a poker-faced Indian, only he didn't get his poker face on fast enough."

"You think he was lying?"

"I think he was trying *not* to lie."

"Same here," Frank said thoughtfully. "But I still like him."

The Hardys arrived at the cottage around noon and found Chet working on his birchbark canoe. It lay overturned on the ground in front of the cabin.

"How're you coming along, Chet?" Joe asked.

"Great! It's almost done. Just have to finish sewing these strips of bark together, which isn't easy on the fingers, I might add."

Just then they heard the phone ringing. Frank dashed into the cabin to answer it. The caller was Alena Tabor.

"How would you boys like to come on a picnic?" she asked.

"Sounds great!" Frank replied. "When and where?"

"Soon as you're ready. I took a chance and told Pokey to pack a lunch for us." Alena suggested a quiet curving branch of the Hawk River, not far from the cottage, as a place to hold the picnic, and described a particularly pleasant spot on the riverbank where she would meet the boys.

"I'd better confess right now that I have an ulterior motive for suggesting this picnic," she added, lowering her voice. "Something has come up that you should know about. We can talk privately at this spot I've picked, without running the risk of someone snooping on our conversation."

"Smart idea. We'll be there," Frank promised.

Chet was in a dilemma when he heard about the invitation. Although eager for another chance to see his new dream girl, he was also desperately anxious to finish his canoe.

The stout youth stood scratching his head for a moment, with a look of frustration on his freckled moonface and perspiration glistening on his tubby torso. "Listen," he said finally, "you go ahead, and I'll join you as soon as I can."

"Okay," the Hardys agreed.

"Just one thing," Chet added as they turned away.

"What's that?" Joe asked.

"Don't start lunch till I get there!"

The boys hiked to the picnic spot and found Alena waiting for them on the bank of the sparkling stream with her red miniwagon parked nearby. She wore jeans and a pretty embroidered cotton blouse and was holding a copy of the local paper, the *Hawk River Herald*.

"Big news?" Joe inquired.

"Bad news, I'm afraid. At least it's not very pleasant from my family's standpoint." She handed him the paper.

Frank and Joe saw its banner headline: "ANOTHER WEREWOLF ATTACK!" But Alena pointed to a different story, splashed all over the front page. It was a lengthy report of the Tabor family's werewolf tradition, and pointed out that young Tabor was a seventh-generation descendant of the last alleged werewolf, Jan Tabor. This, the story implied, automatically made him a prime suspect in the local outbreak of lycanthropy.

"That's a shame," Frank said with a sympathetic frown when he finished reading. "But I'm not really surprised."

Alena's eyebrows went up. "What do you mean?"

"That nasty little werewolf masquerade at your barbecue yesterday evening. Whoever was wearing that outfit was limping as if he'd been shot in the leg—like your ancestor, Jan Tabor."

"So you noticed, too!"

Frank nodded. "The author of a book on werewolves told us about those oldtime cases. And if someone here at Hawk River has found out about your ancestor, and was malicious enough to play that prank last night, it seemed pretty likely the story would soon get around."

64

"Can you imagine how all the neighbors will be talking now?" Alena said unhappily. "If people start picking on John or he imagines they suspect him, I hate to think how he'll react. I'm afraid he'll end up in a worse state than ever!"

The Hardys tried to comfort the girl as best they could. Luckily, there was soon a distraction to take her mind off the subject. Frank and Joe saw her eyes widen, and she pointed toward the stream.

"Look!" she exclaimed.

A majestic figure clad in a buckskin hunting shirt was paddling toward them in a birchbark canoe.

"It's Chet!" Joe cried out.

Their beefy chum made a striking sight in his wilderness costume as he swung his dripping paddle from one side of the canoe to the other.

"He's even wearing an Indian headband!" Frank muttered.

Chet was sitting rigidly upright like a stalwart mountain man or impassive redskin brave. Presently he paused from paddling and struck a gazing pose, as if scanning a distant shore for a sign of friend or foe. The Hardys stifled wild chuckles, realizing their pal was doing all this to impress Alena.

Suddenly Frank frowned. "Am I seeing things, or is that canoe getting lower and lower in the water?"

"You're not seeing things," Joe confirmed. "Chet's sinking!"

Both boys realized that their pal must be feeling very

uncomfortable with the water rising higher and higher around his hips. Nevertheless, his chubby face retained its dignified expression, with no sign of panic. The only hint of anxiety was that he began paddling faster and faster.

Could he reach shore before his craft capsized? The Hardys wondered. The answer was soon apparent, however. In a few moments the canoe had sunk practically out of sight! Chet cast his dignity to the wind and tried to leap overboard. Unfortunately his foot caught on the gunwale and he plopped headfirst into the river in a resounding belly flop that sent water splashing high in the air!

The canoe corkscrewed over on one side, upending for a moment, then once again sinking from view. Chet, meanwhile, was flailing the water with his arms and legs, trying to get his bearings and strike out for shore.

Alena had run to the river's edge with Frank and Joe. "Is he all right?" she asked anxiously.

"Sure, no problem," Frank replied. "Chet's the best water polo player at Bayport High."

"But it looks as if he may lose that canoe he sweated so hard over," Joe added.

Without another word, the plump, apple-cheeked girl kicked off her rope-soled espadrilles and dove gracefully into the water.

"For crying out loud," Joe groaned. "She's making us look like backward chumps!"

66

Frank chuckled. "Never mind. They don't need our help."

Apparently the river was about five or six feet deep at this point. Between them, Alena and Chet managed to retrieve the canoe and haul it ashore. The Hardys helped them drag it up on the bank.

Chet was dewy-eyed with gratitude and astonishment that Alena had jumped in to help him. "That's the bravest thing I ever saw!" he blurted.

Alena smiled. "Well, I couldn't let you lose that beautiful canoe your friends say you worked so hard to make," she told him and gave him a consoling kiss on the cheek.

To Chet, all the labor he had put into his canoe had paid off beyond his wildest dreams! He never stopped smiling while he and Frank examined the damage to the craft. Joe and Alena, meanwhile, went off to lay out the picnic lunch.

"Here's your problem," Frank pointed out. "You sewed this row of stitches right in line with the way the bark splits. As a result, the bark is already starting to tear. Same down here. That's probably what caused the leaks. You should have staggered the stitch holes, or else run your stitches across the grain, so to speak."

"Guess you're right," Chet said. "But who cares?" Lowering his voice and glancing over his shoulder, he added, "Boy, hasn't Alena got spunk, though! I think she likes me a little!"

"Could be," Frank said with a straight face.

Pocahontas had packed chicken sandwiches and chocolate cake, and the picnic lunch proved to be a great success, despite the discomfort of Chet's and Alena's wet clothes. Afterwards, Frank steered the conversation back to the werewolf mystery and the feature in the *Hawk River Herald*.

"Any idea how the editor might have gotten hold of all that information?" he inquired.

Alena hesitated, her brow puckering. "As I told you, my father once mentioned it jokingly in a magazine interview—"

"What magazine?"

"*Worldweek*. I suppose the editor of the *Herald* ran across that story. I can't imagine where else he could have learned all those details," Alena said.

"We'll find out," Joe promised.

Frank nodded. "Another thing. Now that this old-time werewolf yarn has come out in the open, I think it's time Joe and I talked directly to your brother. He may know something important."

A worried look flickered over Alena's face. "Is that really necessary? Both Dad and I are afraid it may only make John's delusions worse."

"I don't see why. The very fact that Joe and I are trying to *solve* this mystery should prove to him that we don't take any stock in such superstitions, and we certainly don't believe he himself turns into a werewolf when the moon is full!"

Alena smiled. "Very well, then. How soon would you like to see John?"

"This afternoon, if possible. We can visit the *Herald* editor first and then go out to your place, that is, if your brother is in shape to talk to us. How did he act this morning, by the way?"

"He slept like a log and didn't wake up till noon. He seemed fairly normal, but apparently doesn't remember a thing about what happened last night."

Alena drove the boys back to the cabin with Chet's waterlogged canoe on top of her miniwagon. Then she went home. Meanwhile, the Hardys transferred to their own car and drove into Hawk River, leaving Chet to change into dry clothes.

They found the *Herald's* office on the town's main street. The editor, a red-haired man named Lyle Dunn, recognized them immediately when they introduced themselves as the sons of Fenton Hardy.

"So you're up here to solve our great werewolf mystery!"

"Let's say we'd like to do whatever we can," Frank said evenly. "As you can imagine, that story you printed about the Tabor family is pretty embarrassing to them."

The editor shrugged. "We only print the news."

"What makes you so sure you got your facts right? Apparently you didn't even bother to check them out."

"Didn't need to," said Dunn. "They came from an interview with Karel Tabor himself."

Frank frowned. "You mean the one that appeared in *Worldweek* magazine?"

"Right, and confirmed by additional research data."

69

"Where'd you run across that?" Joe asked.

"I didn't. It was mailed to me." The editor rose from his chair, pulled a manila envelope out of a file drawer, and showed its contents to the boys. One item was a photocopy of the magazine article, and there were several pages of typewritten notes, stapled together. Each bore the printed initials, D.Q., at the top.

Joe whistled in surprise as he saw the latter. "You said these came in the mail. Who was the sender?"

"No idea. As you can see, there was no name on the envelope, or inside it, either. Just an anonymous tip."

"Well, for your information," Frank said, "that typewritten material was stolen from the author Desmond Quorn."

A faint look of alarm passed over the editor's face.

"Furthermore," Frank went on, "if readers get the impression from your story that John Tabor's responsible for these local werewolf attacks, you might be sued for libel."

"I didn't say Tabor was the werewolf!" Dunn defended himself hastily, looking more alarmed than ever.

"Maybe not directly, but people would certainly get that idea."

"Why should they? This isn't the Middle Ages. There's no more reason why they should think John Tabor is some kind of wolfman than there is to blame the attacks on one of Alec Virgil's wolves."

"Who's Alec Virgil?" Joe asked.

"A naturalist who runs what he calls a 'wolf farm' near here. He breeds wolves, and some of them run pretty big, too!" The redheaded newsman got up from his desk again and fished some more material from another file drawer. "There's a story I wrote about him a week or two ago."

The Hardys read the clipping with keen interest. It reported how Alec Virgil carried on his project as a labor of love to help preserve the buffalo wolf, a species threatened with extinction. It also showed a photograph of Virgil standing beside the stuffed effigy of one of his earliest pet wolves.

Frank rose from his chair. "Okay, thanks for your time, Mr. Dunn. We appreciate your help."

"My pleasure, boys. Stop in any time."

After leaving the *Herald's* office, the Hardys drove back to the cabin, picked up Chet, and went on to the Tabor home.

Parking their car in the drive, Frank and Joe started up to the front door, with Chet tagging at their heels. Directly above, they could see the burly figure of Pocahontas, the half-breed housekeeper. She was perched on a second-floor sill, washing windows.

Frank hesitated a moment, not sure whether he ought to call up to her or draw her attention with a gentle knock. On the other hand, he reflected, Alena was expecting them and was probably downstairs ready to answer the door. He reached out to ring the bell.

71

His finger had just pressed the button when both he and Joe heard a splashing sound and a muffled gasp and felt something wet splatter them from behind.

Turning around, the Hardys gaped in astonishment. The housekeeper had just dumped her pail of water on Chet!

9

Ghostly Voices

Chet spluttered and gasped, drenched to the skin!

Frank glanced up at Pocahontas, who was leaning outward from the windowsill. From the scowl on her coppery-skinned face, Frank was glad she did not have another pail of water handy. He had a hunch that, otherwise, he and his brother might have gotten the same treatment as Chet!

"Good grief!" muttered Joe, appalled at their stout chum's face. "The poor guy practically drowns before lunch and now gets doused all over again!"

"Serves him right!" growled Pocahontas just as the front door opened. "That'll teach him not to dump my little girl in the river!"

"Pokey!" exclaimed Alena, taking in the scene at one horror-stricken glance. "Chet didn't dump me in the river! His canoe sank and I dived in to help save it!"

"Huh!" The housekeeper tossed her braids defiantly. "Amounts to the same thing! It was on account of him that pretty embroidered blouse of yours got ruined, after all the time I spent this morning, ironing it just so!"

"My blouse isn't ruined!" Alena scolded. "It just got soaked! And another thing, Poca—"

Before she could finish speaking, the housekeeper withdrew from her perch, and the Hardys heard the upstairs window being slammed.

"Oh, brother!" Alena shook her head in vexation and embarrassment. "That bossy old Mohawk! She'll drive me up the wall one of these days." The girl added, "I'm so sorry about this. Come on in, boys, and I'll find some dry clothes for Chet."

The stout youth blushed and mumbled awkwardly, "You d-don't have to go to any trouble, Alena!" He was shivering due to his wetness, but obviously pleased at her concern.

Unfortunately, John Tabor's clothes were too small for Chet's barrel-shaped figure, so Alena dug up an old shirt and a pair of slacks which belonged to her father. After Chet retired to a bathroom to change, it became apparent that they were not a perfect fit, either. But they would have to do until he could get dry clothes of his own back at the cottage.

"Never mind, Chet," said Joe with a sympathetic chuckle. "At least you won't get busted for sneaking around in your underwear!"

74

The Hardys turned as they heard footsteps on the stairs. John was coming down to join them. The young architect looked more alert than he had when he had returned home in the wee hours of the morning, but he was obviously in poor spirits.

He shook hands with the visitors, smiled wanly on hearing about Chet's comical mistreatment at the hands of Pocahontas, then settled himself in a chair.

Frank hesitated, not sure how to begin. Finally he said, "Perhaps you've heard of my father. His name is Fenton Hardy."

John nodded. "The famous detective. Yes, I rather thought you two might be the Hardy boys I've read so much about. I suppose Alena got you up here to get to the bottom of this werewolf mystery."

"I'm glad you call it a mystery," Frank said. "That means you don't believe in those old superstitions about werewolves any more than we do."

John Tabor shrugged unhappily and ran his fingers through his curly brown hair. "Right now I don't know *what* to believe. I can't remember a thing about last night—either where I went or what happened while I was gone."

"But at least you don't think you turned into a wolf and attacked people or animals?" put in Joe. "Your common sense tells you that's impossible?"

"Maybe so," John conceded. "But that doesn't explain what I *did* do. You see, I'm not afraid of turning into a wolf. What worries me is that I may become insane, and, if that happens, I might wind up *acting* like a werewolf!"

"Where did you first get the notion that you might be going out of your mind?" Frank inquired.

"While I was studying for my architect's license. I'd be deep in my books, or bent over the drawing board, and then I'd get these calls—"

"What sort of calls, and from whom?"

"Don't ask me. From people I never heard of before. Maybe people I just made up in some sick part of my mind. I used to imagine they were—they were accusing me of being a werewolf!"

Joe frowned. "How do you know you just imagined it? May be you really did get such calls."

"Sure," said Chet, trying to be helpful. "It could've been someone playing a dirty trick on you!"

Tabor gave another helpless shrug. "Maybe. But I find that pretty hard to accept. Why would anyone want to play such a trick on me?"

"You can't think of anyone?" Frank prodded.

"Nobody at all. I don't have any real enemies. I'm just not that important. Besides, the delusions got even worse after I checked into the sanatorium. I suppose Alena or my father told you about that."

"The sanatorium? Yes, your Dad did mention that you'd gone for treatment, to the Pine Manor Rest Home, I believe. What happened? More calls?"

"No. Just voices."

"From where?" Joe asked.

76

John Tabor rubbed his head in bewilderment at the disturbing recollection. "I don't know. From the walls, I guess, or just out of thin air. I'd hear them in my room, first at night, when I was just drifting off to sleep. Later on, when it got worse, I'd even hear them during the day when I was wide awake."

"What did the voices say?"

"Terrible things, about rending fangs and bloodlust and so on. They said they were the voices of my old werewolf ancestors, like the Jan Tabor who was convicted in Bohemia in 1759."

Seeing that both John and Alena were becoming upset, Frank decided to end the questioning for the time being.

"Look," he said, "would you mind if Joe and I went to that sanatorium and interviewed the doctor who treated you?"

"Of course not," the young architect replied. "If you think it'll help in any way."

"It can't do any harm. But we'll need a letter from you, giving permission to ask questions about your case. And would you write down the name and address of the sanatorium, too, please?"

John nodded and Frank asked for directions to Alec Virgil's wolf farm. After saying good-by to Alena and her brother, the Hardy's drove back to the cabin so Chet could change into dry clothes of his own. Then they took the river road eastward out of town.

The preserve lay spread out on a slope forested with

cedar and hemlock, and was enclosed by a high wire fence. A sign over the gate said:

WOLFVILLE   Alec Virgil, Prop.
Guided Tours $1.00   Please Ring Bell

Joe did, and after a short wait a man drove up in a battered-looking jeep to greet them. He was tall and deeply tanned, with a mane of sandy hair.

"Howdy, boys!" he said, unlocking and opening the gate. "Come to see my lobos?"

"That's right, Mr. Virgil," Frank grinned. "We heard about your place this afternoon. I never knew anyone who actually raised wolves."

"Someone's got to protect the species! In most places everyone's against them. There's a wonderful preserve on the Olympic Peninsula of Washington State, where they breed five times as many wolves as I've got here. Still, I'm doing my bit."

Because of the rough terrain, Virgil suggested the boys ride with him in his jeep. They paid their admission and climbed in.

"Where'd you get your wolves?" Joe asked.

"The original stock came from the Great Plains. They used to run in packs when huge herds of buffalo dotted the plains, but they're all gone now. I bought half a dozen from the descendants of the last few caught by the government trappers in the late 1920s. Now I have thirty-seven."

"Good for you. Must take a lot of work, though."

Virgil laughed. "True. I have to be the general handy-man, the vet, the animal feeder, the yard cleaner-upper, the purchasing agent, and a few other things. But my wife helps me, and we find it a lot more satisfying than the kind of life we used to lead back in the city."

As they drove along, more and more wolves came bounding out from among the trees. Virgil slowed the jeep, and several lobos jogged alongside, their tongues lolling. They were magnificent beasts, ranging in color from silver gray and blond to cinnamon brown. Some were seven feet long from nose to hind legs.

At one point, Alec Virgil stopped the jeep and got out to play with his charges. They surged around him, wild with delight at the chance for a romp. He wrestled with them and even rolled on the ground while they nipped playfully at his arms or legs, yet never doing him any harm with their huge jaws and fearsome-looking teeth.

"Are they—er, dangerous?" Chet asked.

"Yes and no," Mr. Virgil replied. "Most of the stories about wolves attacking men are nonsense. They're actually shy creatures. But they're not lapdogs, either. They should be *respected*."

The boys decided to stay in the jeep. They found the wolves' yellow-eyed stares a bit disconcerting. Finally Virgil drove to his house and invited the guests in for coffee. When he found out that Frank and Joe were the sons of the famous Fenton Hardy, he wanted to refund their admission. But the boys refused, knowing from

79

Alena that the naturalist was often hard-pressed to keep his farm going.

Mrs. Virgil, a smiling, motherly woman, served coffee and doughnuts, then went outside. While the boys sat around the fireplace, her husband told them more about the sad story of the plains wolves.

"When hunters killed off the buffalo herds and thinned out the elk and antelope and deer populations," he related, "many wolves starved. Others took to preying on livestock. So the ranchers and settlers went after them with poison and traps. It was a long, desperate duel. The wolves learned to refuse the poisoned bait and became incredibly cunning at avoiding traps. But finally the humans won, and the lobos disappeared from the plains."

As he finished speaking, the distant howl of a wolf was heard from outside, then others joined in. The boys were thrilled by the eerie chorus. But gradually it changed to wilder yelping and barking.

Alec Virgil rose from his chair in alarm. Just then his wife hurried in, her face pale with excitement.

"Someone's cut the fence wire!" she cried. "Our wolves are getting out!"

10

Skyscraper Caper

"What part of the fence?" Virgil asked his wife.

When she told him, he moved into action swiftly, like a man used to handling such crises. He slipped a small whistle into his pocket, got some meat from a freezer in the shed, then climbed behind the wheel of his jeep. With the boys accompanying him, he careened off through the trees toward the section of cut fence.

Some of the wolves, more cautious than dogs might have been, were merely nosing around and sniffing at the freedom that lay beyond the opening. Others had already plunged through and were exploring the brush along the road.

Virgil leaped out of the jeep and blew his whistle. Even though it did not make a sound audible to the

82

human ear, the escaped wolves instantly turned and loped toward the enclosure—slowly at first, then faster and faster as he waved handfuls of meat in the air. Soon he was the center of a frenzied mass of leaping, snapping lobos. Virgil flung the meat in several directions, but all of it away from the fence. The pack raced off, each animal eager to fight for his share.

Satisfied that all his wolves were accounted for, Virgil hastily moved the jeep so as to block any further escape through the hole in the fence. Then, using tools and wire from a repair kit mounted on the back of the vehicle, he and the boys wired the ripped fencing back in place. There was no doubt that it had been cut deliberately.

"Who'd do such a thing?" Frank asked.

"You'd be surprised," Virgil said wryly. "I've had all sorts of trouble ever since I started my wolf farm. Most people hate wolves and think they should all be wiped out."

"Maybe they would be, if it weren't for people like you and your wife," said Joe.

Alec Virgil smiled and nodded. "Yep, Mary and I love the critters. When the mother wolves bring out their pups to show us every spring, the little ones are rather like our own grandchildren."

He explained that the she-wolves burrowed underground dens in which to raise their litters. At night, the wolf "families" were kept in separate pens or runs, instead of ranging freely over the whole preserve.

"Which gives you double protection against a break-out?" Joe remarked.

"That's right. Good thing, too, with this werewolf foolishness going on. I don't intend to give people around here any excuse to blame those so-called werewolf attacks on my critters!"

"How come we didn't hear that whistle you blew?" Chet asked as they drove back to the house. "Was it ultrasonic?"

"Yep, it's inaudible to human ears, but my lobos hear it! Usually it's the signal for feeding time, but they're trained to respond any time I whistle."

"Hey!" Frank suddenly snapped his fingers. "That may explain it!"

"Explain what?" Joe inquired.

"What happened Saturday night at the Bayport Diner! Look, Mr. Virgil blew that ultrasonic whistle for his wolves to come, and he used the meat as an extra scent lure."

"So?" Joe looked puzzled.

"Maybe that phony werewolf we saw was trained like an attack dog, and its owner swiped my jacket as a scent guide to clue it in to our group!"

"I'll bet you're right!" said Joe, catching on. "He let the animal sniff your jacket so it would know to attack you when we came out of the diner. Then Chet and the others rushed to help us, and he blew an ultrasonic whistle to call his critter back."

"What are you talking about?" Alec Virgil asked.

After they went into the house again to finish their

84

doughnuts and coffee, they explained what had happened, and Virgil agreed that Frank's theory was a very likely one. Joe inquired about the stuffed wolf that had been shown in the newspaper photo. "I don't see it anywhere," the boy remarked.

"I sold it—or *thought* I did," Alec Virgil replied. "Turned out to be just another dirty trick."

He explained that he had received a phone call after the picture appeared in the *Hawk River Herald*. The caller, pretending to be a wealthy donor, said he wanted to buy the wolf and present it as a gift to the Mountain View Natural History Museum.

"That lobo had been a special pet of Mary's and mine," Virgil went on, "and we hated to part with it. But the caller offered us a thousand dollars."

Since the wolf farm existed on occasional grants and donations from animal lovers and the admission fees paid by sightseers, meeting the monthly bills was often a struggle. So the couple finally agreed to sell their beloved specimen.

"A truck came and picked it up," Virgil told the boys, "and the driver left a check which turned out to be worthless. When I called the museum, the curator knew nothing about it and said he had never received the wolf."

Later, back at the cabin, the boys were about to sit down to an early supper when the telephone rang. Joe answered and recognized Hank Eagle's voice.

"Hi, Hank," he said cordially. "Where are you calling from?"

"New York City. I flew back at lunchtime in Mr. Tabor's helicopter. He told me where you're staying."

The Mohawk explained that, during the afternoon, he had rejoined his regular high-steel construction crew working on the Manhattan skyscraper which Chelsea Builders were erecting.

"And I spotted something I think you ought to see," Hank went on. "It may be important to that case your father's investigating. Could you come to New York right away?"

"You mean tonight?"

"Yes. Something may happen here that you'll want to keep an eye on."

Joe checked with Frank, and they decided to follow Hank's suggestion. He gave them precise instructions on where to meet him. Then the boys called Bayport to inform their father, only to learn that he was gone for the evening. However, their mother told them that they had received an anonymous phone message about three o'clock."

"It was a man," she reported. "He said he was the person with dark glasses whom you saw at Eagle's Nest this morning."

"What did he want?" Frank asked excitedly.

"He wants to meet you. Call 555-3621 and ask for Mr. Nest. The area code is 212."

"Thanks for the info, Mom," Frank said and hung up.

"It's a New York number," Joe pointed out. "That fits in nicely with our trip tonight."

"Right," Frank agreed, and dialed the number. An answering service responded, but the operator was unable to arrange a meeting. "Mr. Nest," she said, "calls in every so often to see if there's any word from the Hardy boys. In fact, I heard from him just about twenty minutes ago, so I don't know how soon he'll call again."

"Okay," Frank said. "If he checks in, tell him we'll be in New York tonight. I'll contact you again around ten o'clock."

After a hasty meal, the Hardys started the long drive to New York, leaving a somewhat nervous Chet to keep watch on the Tabors' house after dark. Dusk had fallen as they sped southward on the New York State Thruway, and it was well past nine when they arrived in Manhattan. They parked in a midtown lot, as Hank Eagle had suggested, and walked a block or so to the meeting place.

The Mohawk was waiting for them in a doorway across the street from the skyscraper which was under construction by Chelsea Builders. He quickly told the boys the reason for his call.

"Just before I quit working," Hank said, "I noticed a lunch box stashed against a girder."

"You mean somewhere high up on the building skeleton?" Joe asked.

"Right. The twenty-first floor to be exact. Often, when the men are working, they don't bother coming down to the street for lunch. Anyhow, I figured one of the construction crew must've forgotten it when he left.

So I opened it thinking there might be something in it to clue me in to whom it belonged." Hank shook his head as if still slightly incredulous. "Boy, you'll never guess what I found inside!"

"Something suspicious?" Frank suggested.

"You better believe it! There was a drawing like a building floor plan, with an X mark and some numbers. At first I thought it might have something to do with the skyscraper we're working on, but then, as I looked at it closely, I realized that it was a layout of our company offices on Seventh Avenue!"

"What about the X mark?" Joe questioned.

"That's what made me call you. It indicated the location of the company safe! Those numbers were probably the combination. What's more, there was also a key in the lunch box, perhaps to the outside door of the office suite!"

Joe whistled. "Wow! That sounds like a preparation for a robbery—an inside job! But who could have left the lunch box? Any idea?"

Hank related that a group of company officials had visited the structure that very afternoon. "Some had on loose cotton dust coats, so one of them might have smuggled up the lunch box and left it, or at least stashed the paper and key if the box was already planted there. Then, tonight when it's dark, maybe the crook who'll pull the robbery is supposed to pick it up!"

"Smart thinking, Hank, " Frank agreed. "That could be their plan, all right."

"And the guys who set it up," Joe added, "may also be involved in those three Chelsea building cases Dad's investigating!"

"Right, which is why I tipped you two off," said the Indian high-steel worker. "But what do we do about it?"

The Hardys exchanged thoughtful glances.

"Think we should warn Mr. Tabor?" Joe asked his brother. "After all, he's the head of the company."

"I know," Frank said, deciding to trust the Mohawk and speak openly in front of him. "But we still can't be sure he himself isn't mixed up in all this. Was he one of the company officials who came here today to inspect the structure?"

Hank nodded ruefully. "I'm afraid he was."

"Looks as if we'll have to play it by ear, then, and use our own judgment," Frank decided.

"How do we know the lunch box is still there?" Joe asked.

The Mohawk shrugged. "We don't. I've been hanging around here ever since it got dark, trying to keep my eyes peeled for anything suspicious, but that doesn't prove much. Maybe we'd better check."

"Isn't there a watchman on duty?" Frank inquired.

"Sure, but he's a lazy bum. Spends most of the time with his feet up, reading the paper. Anyone could sneak by him."

"Okay then, if it won't stir up any trouble, let's have a look!"

89

The skyscraper was going up between two other buildings. The base of its structural skeleton was enclosed by a high board fence. After cautious glances to see whether the coast was clear, the three darted across the street. Hank Eagle gave each of the Hardys a boost up the fence, then leaped for a handhold and swung over easily by himself.

In a lighted booth just inside the access doorway through the fence, they could see the watchman snoring with a newspaper on his lap and a thermos of coffee on the table next to him.

"See what I mean?" Hank grinned.

"How do we get to the twenty-first floor?" Joe inquired.

"There's a freight hoist, but it makes a lot of noise when you switch on the motor. It'd probably wake even *him* up. Better walk."

Temporary wooden stairways had been erected for the workmen, leading up through the building skeleton. The Hardys and their Mohawk friend felt leaden-legged as they neared their destination in spite of their trim physical condition.

Suddenly they heard a metallic clink in the darkness. "Hold it!" Hank Eagle hissed, putting a hand on each boy's arm.

They were ascending a connecting stairway on the right side of the structure. Peering outward and upward, they discovered that someone had heaved a line from a window of the adjoining building to hook onto the floor of the skyscraper skeleton somewhere above them. As they watched, they could see the dark figure of a man silhouetted in the moonlight, shinnying his way up from the window along the rope.

"I'll bet he's going after the lunch box!" Joe whispered.

"Right! Let's get him!" Frank urged.

All three dashed up the stairs on tiptoe. As they reached the twenty-first floor, they saw the intruder scramble over the edge and onto the temporary flooring of the skyscraper. Then he darted silently across the wooden planks.

"That's what he's after, all right!" Hank muttered to the boys. "The lunch box is over that way!"

They moved to cut off the stranger's retreat to the hook and line. But evidently he heard them. With a fleeting glance over his shoulder, he ran nimbly over an open girder toward another part of the structure. The very thought of his reckless flight, hundreds of feet above the ground, made the Hardys dizzy.

Hank Eagle set off after him without hesitation. "Wait—don't try it, you two!" he told the Hardys as he dashed over the girder in pursuit. "Leave this to me!"

Watching the two figures intently in the moonlit gloom, the brothers saw the fugitive reach another stairway. Instead of heading downward to street level, he started up, bounding two or three steps at a stride.

"Keep an eye on him while I try to cut him off!" Joe blurted and darted back to the stairway they them-

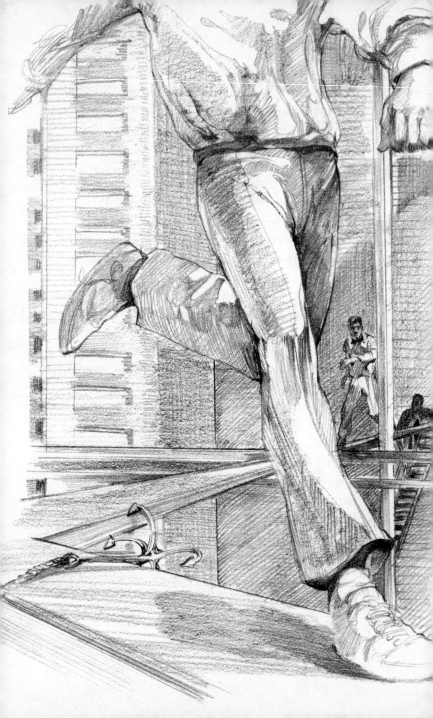

selves had used. Construction on the skyscraper had progressed only three stories higher, with the unfinished skeleton ending on the twenty-fourth floor.

As he reached it, Joe caught sight of the intruder, who was running across the wooden planking toward the edge of the structure. Joe sensed his intention at a glance. He was going to leap down onto the roof of the adjoining building from which he had emerged only a few minutes before!

The Hardy boy rushed to stop him. He grabbed the fugitive by the arm. But the man broke loose with a muttered oath. They grappled wildly at the brink of the planking. Too late, Joe saw the man's fist swinging at him in the moonlight.

The blow caught him on the side of the head and he lost his balance. With a startled cry, Joe toppled into the yawning darkness below!

11

Xavier's Story

Plummeting downward, Joe saw a rope flash past his eyes. He grabbed it desperately, and the jerk on his arm confirmed that his fall had been broken.

As he collected his wits, Joe realized he had managed to grab hold of the line which the intruder had hooked onto the skyscraper.

What a lucky break! Joe thought. With a prayer of thanks on his lips, he got a two-handed grip on the line. Then he swung his legs around the rope as a further safety measure and made his way downward cautiously, hand over hand.

The line slanted outward, away from the skyscraper skeleton into the adjoining building. As Joe shinnied down the rope and wriggled through the window, a new thought occurred to him.

Perhaps the contents of the room he was now in would enable him to identify the unknown intruder or maybe indicate whom he worked for, if others were involved.

But when Joe groped along the wall and found a light switch, he was disappointed. The room was empty, evidently an unrented office. The line had been tied to a radiator underneath the window. Hastily he switched off the light again so as not to make a target of himself.

"Better not stick my head out the window, either," Joe reflected. The safest way would be to go down to the street and wait for Frank and Hank Eagle.

Luckily the building corridors were still lighted and the elevators were working. A night attendant glanced at Joe curiously as he stepped into the lobby, but said nothing.

Joe went out into the street and was greeted with excited relief by his brother and their Mohawk friend a moment or two later.

"Thank goodness you're okay!" Frank exclaimed, putting an arm around his brother's shoulder. "Boy, I thought you were a goner when I saw you go over the side!"

"I never even got a good look at the guy before he punched me," Joe grumbled. "What happened to him?"

"He jumped on the roof of the building you went into," Frank reported, "and then took off via the fire escape."

"Well, at least he didn't get what he came for," Hank Eagle added, displaying the lunch box. The paper and key were still inside it.

"That's a break!" Joe said with satisfaction. "Whatever he and his pals were up to, we seem to have spoiled their plans."

"Right," Frank agreed. "So I guess we don't have to worry about warning anyone till we get a chance to talk to Dad." He looked at his watch. "But maybe we should give Mr. Nest another ring."

When he dialed the number from a nearby phone booth, the answering-service operator said there had been no further word from their mysterious caller. Frank promised to check again the following day and hung up. Hank Eagle invited the boys to stay overnight at his apartment in the Manhattan neighborhood known as the East Village, and they gladly accepted.

Next morning, Frank phoned Bayport. Fenton Hardy answered. When he learned his son was calling from New York City, the detective exclaimed, "Great! You couldn't have timed it better!"

"How come, Dad?"

"I've just had word from the insurance underwriters that the offices of Chelsea Builders were broken into last night. The safe was cracked and looted. I'd like you and Joe to go there and get a full report."

Frank was startled by the news. When he related their adventure on the skyscraper skeleton, Mr. Hardy agreed with Hank Eagle's suspicions. "I'd say last night's burglary proves your Mohawk friend was right. The crooks probably had to break in and crack the safe because you fellows stopped them from getting the key and combination."

The detective said he expected to leave the house shortly to pursue his investigation. So rather than phone back, Frank promised that he and Joe would stop off in Bayport before returning to the Adirondacks and report what they had learned about the burglary.

Chelsea Builders were located in an office building on Seventh Avenue near 38th Street. The Hardys found the premises swarming with police and newsmen. After identifying themselves as the sons of the famed private detective who had been retained by the firm's insurance underwriters, they were admitted at once to the office of the president, Karel Tabor.

With him was a younger man, whom Mr. Tabor introduced as his executive assistant, Neal Xavier. Tabor's manner seemed rather curt and worried.

"Can you tell us what was taken from the safe, sir?" Frank asked.

"Luckily less than a thousand dollars. Just the usual petty cash that we keep on hand."

"Anything else of special value?" Joe inquired.

Mr. Tabor looked slightly uncomfortable. "We—er—don't have an exact list of the safe's contents just yet. The treasurer's secretary is compiling one," he replied, then stole a hasty glance at his wristwatch. "Look, if you'll excuse me, I have a rather urgent appointment to attend to. Perhaps Mr. Xavier here can answer any other questions you may have."

The Hardys refrained from showing their surprise. "Whatever you say, sir," Frank said politely.

Neal Xavier, a sharp-eyed, hawk-nosed man with dark hair, conducted the boys into his own office next door and invited them to be seated.

"You're probably wondering why Mr. Tabor had so little to say," he began, sitting down behind his desk. "Well, he had his reasons."

The Hardys waited for Xavier to explain.

"The fact is, he suspects another firm of architects may have had a hand in the robbery," the executive aide went on, "namely, Upton Associates. But Mr. Tabor feels it's unethical to make any accusations without proof."

Xavier thumped his fist angrily on the desk and added, "Well, I can tell you right now that won't stop *me* from speaking out. I think a crook is a crook and deserves whatever happens to him!"

"Assuming you're both right," said Joe, "that Upton Associates *are* crooks, why would they want to rob your safe?"

"Very simple," Xavier replied. "For some time now, my boss has suspected Upton of taking illegal kickbacks and bribes."

"From whom?" said Frank with a frown.

"From a crooked contractor with mob connections. Whenever Upton Associates designs buildings, they use their influence to see that that particular contractor gets hired to do the work, even though they know his firm is partly run by gangsters."

"And in return," Joe said, "you mean the crooked contractor hands some of the money he is paid for the job back to Upton Associates?"

"Right. Under the table, as they say. Since the contractor overcharges the customer, he can afford to return a share of the take to Upton. It so happens Mr. Tabor's been collecting secret testimony about such payoffs on tape. But now those tapes are missing from the safe!"

Before leaving, the Hardys asked if they could look at the company safe. Its door was hanging loosely by the hinges.

"Expert job," Joe remarked to his brother. "Evidently the safecracker used just enough nitro to blow it open without damaging anything else."

Frank nodded and knelt down to scrape some shreds of pinkish substance off the metal with his fingernail. He sniffed it and pulled it apart.

Joe puckered his forehead. "What is it?"

"Believe it or not, it's chewing gum!"

As the Hardy boys left the Chelsea Builders suite of offices and started down the corridor toward the elevators, they suddenly heard footsteps darting up behind them.

The next moment, each felt something jabbed in his back and a voice snarled, "Hold it, you two!"

12

Restaurant Meeting

Frank and Joe whirled around. From the speaker's snarling tone, they expected to find a hard-eyed gunman behind them.

Instead, they saw a smiling, freckle-faced young man in his early twenties. He held up a pen in one hand and a keychain flashlight in the other.

"Excuse the funny stuff, fellows," he apologized. "Just wanted to make sure you didn't get away. You two are the famous Hardy boys, aren't you?"

"That's right," Frank said.

"I'm Matt Dawson of the *Daily Star*. Just new on the job, to tell you the truth. But I'd sure like to impress the city editor, and getting an interview with you guys would be a step in the right direction. How about it?"

The Hardys exchanged dubious glances. Then Frank shook his head. "Thanks, but we'd rather not."

"Are you or your father working on this case?"

"If we were, we couldn't talk about it."

"Look, that doesn't matter. You wouldn't have to discuss the Chelsea Builders burglary," the young reporter assured them. "Just an interview for a general feature story will do. Things like how you first got interested in solving mysteries; whether or not you expect to become professional detectives like your father; how your sleuthing fits in with your schoolwork, and so on."

Frank hesitated. After consulting briefly with his brother, he said, "Okay, it's a deal, if you'll do us a favor in return."

"Sure thing, if I can. What do you have in mind?"

"The *Star* is one of the city's biggest newspapers, I believe," Frank said. "You cover all the arts, don't you, including architecture?"

"You bet! We've got as big an editorial staff as any paper in town, and one of the best in the country. A man named Earl Bruce writes a regular column on architecture in the *Sunday Star*."

"Fine. We'll give you an interview if you can persuade him to give us some information in exchange."

Dawson grinned. "You've got it, fellows!"

The Hardys accompanied the reporter several blocks through midtown Manhattan to the *Star* building. Once there, Matt Dawson called the paper's architectural critic on an office phone to confirm the bargain. Frank and Joe were then interviewed and photographed for half an hour. Afterward, Dawson took them to Earl Bruce's office on another floor of the building and left the two to talk to the editor in private.

"Well, boys, what is it you want to know?" the genial, white-haired newsman inquired.

"First of all, sir," Frank requested, "we'd like you to keep this conversation in strict confidence, if you don't mind."

"Agreed."

"Thanks. To get right to the point, then, what can you tell us about an architectual firm called Upton Associates?"

"Hm." Bruce leaned back in his chair and began filling his pipe thoughtfully. "Well, they've been in practice for about fifteen years, as I recall. Do quite a sizable volume of business. Commercial stuff, mostly. Office buildings, factories, that sort of thing. Plus several bridges and occasional government projects."

"Who runs the firm?" Joe put in.

"A man named Zachary Upton."

"What's he like?"

A quirky grin shaped itself on Bruce's lips. "Let's say he's a man of strong individuality."

"Has there ever been any trouble between Upton and Chelsea Builders?" Frank asked.

"Not trouble, exactly, but I believe there has been considerable rivalry between them. I know they've often put in competing bids on the same job; no doubt that may have led to a certain amount of hard feelings. After all, they can't both win out on the same project."

"Have Upton Associates ever been accused of anything crooked or illegal?"

Bruce, who was just lighting his pipe, looked up sharply at Frank's question. "Not that I know of, although I believe Upton has a son who was convicted of some crime and sent to prison."

"On what charge?"

The white-haired newsman thought hard for a few moments, then shook his head. "I'm afraid I don't recall. It didn't happen here in New York City. I just heard it mentioned in a conversation."

After a few more questions, the Hardys thanked Earl Bruce for his help and left the office. In the lobby, Frank paused near a pay telephone.

"Maybe we should try to get in touch with Mr. Nest again," he suggested.

"Good idea," Joe agreed.

Frank slipped a coin into the instrument and dialed the number. When the answering service replied, he asked if Mr. Nest had checked in yet.

"Let me see," the operator replied and consulted her notes. "Yes, he called this morning and suggested meeting you at the Soup Bowl restaurant on East 49th Street. He said he'd contact me again at eleven-thirty to see if you'd gotten the message."

103

"Good enough," said Frank. "Tell him we'll be there."

Hanging up, the boy glanced at his watch. It was now ten minutes after eleven, so the Hardys decided to go directly to the restaurant and have an early lunch. After looking up the address in the phone book, they hailed a taxi, which deposited them in front of the Soup Bowl a few minutes later.

The restaurant was already quite busy, but the brothers found a vacant booth and ordered hamburgers and French fries. While they were waiting to be served, Frank mused. "I wonder if that gum on the safe got there strictly by accident, or if it may not tell us something more."

"Good question," said Joe. "You think it might have turned up on other jobs the guy's pulled?"

Frank nodded thoughtfully. One of the first principles of detection that the Hardys had learned from their father was that a crook's *modus operandi*, or operating procedure, was often the best way to identify the person responsible for a given crime.

"You may have something there," Joe said. "Why don't you call Sam Radley? There's a phone booth over by the counter. You might catch him in if he's not working with Dad today."

"Good idea." Frank got up and placed a long-distance call to Bayport.

Sam Radley was one of Fenton Hardy's top operatives. As it turned out, he was writing a report at his desk and answered immediately. "What can I do for you, Frank?"

"I'm calling from New York, Sam. I wonder if you could check the files and see if you have anything on a safecracker whose known habits include leaving traces of chewing gum on the safe."

Sam chuckled. "I don't have to look. It so happens your Dad wanted a rundown on the same crook recently, in connection with his investigation of those three building disasters."

"No kidding!" Frank felt a surge of excitement.

"The guy in question is a young fellow, a regular technical and electronic whiz," Radley went on. "Got out of prison not long ago. He has a habit of chewing bubble gum while he's working on a job."

"And sometimes the bubbles burst and gum splatters the safe?"

"Right. That's how he got his nickname 'Bubbles'. His real name is Lew Upton."

"Thanks a lot, Sam!" Frank hung up and hurried back to pass on the information to his brother.

The waitress had brought their orders, and Joe was already munching a hamburger. "*Upton?*" he echoed with his mouth still half full. "He could be Zachary Upton's son!"

"Check! The one who was convicted and sent to prison!" Frank said.

The two discussed the latest development eagerly as they ate lunch. Then Frank happened to glance toward the door. He signaled to Joe and said in a low tone, "Here comes our man!"

The mysterious eavesdropper who called himself Mr. Nest had just entered the restaurant and was approaching their table. Gray-haired, with a rather shrunken, wrinkled face, he was wearing sunglasses as before and an expensive-looking bronze silk suit.

"So you kept our appointment. That's good!" he remarked hoarsely, sliding into the booth beside Joe. "Maybe we can do business."

"What kind of business?" Frank asked cooly.

"Don't stall around, Sonny!" the elderly man rasped. "I've got just one thing to discuss with you, and that's the tomahawk! Can we work out a deal or can't we?"

The Hardys stared at him, puzzled. They had no idea what Mr. Nest was talking about.

"First you'd better tell us what tomahawk," Joe demanded, fishing for information.

Instead of answering, however, Mr. Nest leaped up from the booth and hurried out of the restaurant!

13

Toy Boat Trick

"Hey, wait!" Joe called, but the gray-haired mystery man had disappeared before the boys recovered from their surprise.

"Come on, let's go after him!" Frank exclaimed, springing to his feet.

He dashed toward the door, but as he passed the counter, the cashier reached out and grabbed his arm. "Just a minute!" she protested indignantly. "You can't sneak out of here without paying!"

Frank started to explain, but saw that it would be useless, so he fished money out of his pocket and hastily settled their bill.

Meanwhile, Joe brushed past him to pursue Mr. Nest. As he ran out the door, a cane was suddenly thrust in front of him. Joe tripped and sprawled full-length on the pavement!

Angrily he got up and turned to let off steam at the person responsible for the mishap. Then he saw that the cane was held by a poorly dressed man clutching a tin cup with pencils, evidently a blind beggar.

"Sorry if I got in your way," the man mumbled.

Joe stifled the angry remark that had risen to his lips. "Never mind," he said, and hastily collected himself to renew the pursuit. His eyes swept the throng of passing pedestrians and picked out a gray-haired man in a bronze-colored suit near the next corner, about to cross the street.

Joe dashed after him, shouldering his way deftly through the crowd, muttering apologies whenever he bumped into someone. He reached the curb and started across just as the light was changing. With a blare of horns, a pack of cars surged into motion and roared straight at him in the typical impatient fashion of New York traffic.

Joe leaped and hopped across the street, dodging a taxi, a station wagon, and a delivery van. His pulse was racing as he reached the opposite corner but there was no time to stop and cool his jangled nerves. He could see the man in the brownish suit not far ahead.

Joe darted and swivel-hipped his way through the stream of pedestrians. He reached his quarry and grabbed him by the arm. "Okay, Mr. Nest, if that's your real name. Hold it!"

The man turned. He had a large, red nose, veiny jowls, and bushy-browed blue eyes, which at the moment were sparking dangerously. "Let go of my arm, young fellow!" he growled. "Just who do you think you are?"

Joe's eyes widened in chagrin as he saw his mistake. "I—I'm terribly sorry," he stuttered. "I thought you were someone else."

"Hmmph!" The man grunted. "Next time don't grab people before you see who they are!"

Apparently mollified by Joe's apology, he strode off. The younger Hardy plodded back dejectedly toward the restaurant. Crossing the street, he encountered his brother.

"Any luck?" Frank inquired.

"Yes, all of it bad!" Joe said wryly and related his two brief adventures. As if to rub in his humiliation, he saw that the man with the cane had disappeared. "I'll bet that blind beggar was just a phony!" Joe blurted. "Nest probably planted him there to slow us down, in case we came after him."

"Very likely," Frank agreed. "Nest's name is phony, too, for that matter."

"Sure, from the name of that old wooden mansion where you spotted him, Eagle's Nest!"

"Well, never mind, Joe. We can't win 'em all. Let's go back and finish our hamburgers."

But another letdown was in store. When they returned to the restaurant, they saw that their table had already been cleared. The rest of their meal was probably in the garbage by now.

Even Frank was disgusted. "Want to order something else?" he asked his brother.

"Forget it. I just lost my appetite."

Frank decided to use the phone booth again. He called Chelsea Builders and asked Karel Tabor's secretary for the name and address of the client for whom the firm was restoring Eagle's Nest.

Frank jotted down the information she gave him, then hung up and turned to Joe. "Let's look him up when we get a chance. He might be able to give us a lead on Mr. Nest."

"Good hunch. But what'll we do right now?"

"Call Zachary Upton and ask for an interview. Not here, though. Let's go to a place where I can carry on a phone conversation without all this babble and clatter of dishes."

In the lobby of an office building down the street, they found a pay telephone in a quiet, secluded corner. Joe leafed through the Manhattan directory for Upton Associates, and Frank dialed the number. Luckily the head of the firm had not yet gone to lunch, and by quiet persistence, Frank finally got through to him.

"My name's Frank Hardy, Mr. Upton," he began. "My father is Fenton Hardy, the detective. You may have heard of him."

"Well, what is it you want?" the rumbling bass voice challenged.

"My brother Joe and I would like a chance to talk to you, as soon as possible."

"What about?"

"A case which our father's investigating. It involves Chelsea Builders."

"Nothing doing," the architect replied grumpily. "We have no contact with that firm."

"You may still be able to help us, sir."

"I said nothing doing!"

"Very well," Frank said, and on a sudden impulse added, "Then may I speak to your son Lew?"

There was a slight pause, and Frank sensed that Zachary Upton had been taken aback by the sudden mention of his son's name. "He's not here," Upton finally responded.

"Can you tell us how to get in touch with him?"

"This isn't a secretarial bureau—I'm running a firm of architects!"

Frank decided to apply a little pressure. His voice hardened. "It's very important that we speak to Bubbles," he said, emphasizing the nickname slightly. "We want to question him about a burglary that occurred at Chelsea Builders last night. The safe was cracked."

Frank could hear a faint gasp at the other end of the line. "A s-safecracking, you say?"

"That's right, Mr. Upton. My brother and I went there this morning and examined the scene of the burglary. We discovered a clue that *may* link your son to the crime. Now, we'd like to give him a chance to

111

explain. However, if you prefer, we can simply call the police and let *them* follow up."

"No, er, don't do that just yet!" Zachary Upton said hastily. "If you'll call back in half an hour, I'll do my best to arrange an interview with my son."

"Fine. Thank you, sir," Frank said politely. Hanging up he turned to his brother with a dry grin. "That changed his tune in a hurry!"

While waiting to phone back, the Hardys returned to the skyscraper from which Joe had taken his terrifying tumble the night before. The construction crew were still on their lunch break, as the two young sleuths had hoped, so they were able to have a brief chat with their friend, Hank Eagle.

Joe described their frustrating meeting with the so-called Mr. Nest. As he mentioned the man's strange remark about the tomahawk, Frank saw Hank's eyes flicker, as if he were startled but trying not to show any sign of recognition.

"Any idea what the man was talking about?" the older Hardy boy inquired casually.

Hank Eagle shrugged. "None."

For the rest of the conversation he seemed rather taciturn and withdrawn, masking whatever was going on in his head behind a deadpan face.

"Did you notice how Hank clammed up all of a sudden when you asked him about that tomahawk?" Joe remarked to his brother later as they walked away from the construction site.

112

"I'll say I did," Frank replied. "He knows more than he's telling us, that's for sure."

"But why? You don't suppose he's in cahoots with Mr. Nest?"

Frank shook his head. "That doesn't stack up with what we know about Hank, not with our previous opinion of him, anyhow. I've got a hunch about why Mr. Nest set up a meeting with us and tossed out that crack about the tomahawk."

"Why?"

"He wanted to find out from our expressions if we *knew* anything about it. When he saw our blank faces, he realized we didn't, and that's all he was interested in. So he took off and left us sitting there like dummies."

"That figures, all right," Joe agreed.

At a nearby drugstore, Frank made another call to Upton Associates. This time Zachary Upton was much less hostile. He was still vague and uncertain about arranging a meeting between the Hardys and his son. However, he agreed readily to see the boys himself and discuss the matter further.

"I'd like to keep this confidential," he added. "Could we meet somewhere away from my office?"

"You name the time and place, Mr. Upton," Frank said.

"Very well, then. How about two-thirty this afternoon, at the boat pond in Central Park?" The architect added directions, in case the Hardys were not familiar

113

with the layout of the park, and a description of himself.

"We'll be there," Frank promised and hung up.

The boys had left their car overnight in a parking garage, so after some window-shopping on Fifth Avenue, they took a bus north and went into Central Park at the East 72nd Street entrance.

The pond at which they were to meet Upton lay just a short stroll away. The architect was easily identifiable from the description of himself that he had given Frank, a big, shaggy bear of a man with a closely trimmed dark beard streaked with gray.

Several toy boats were being sailed on the pond. As the boys approached, they realized that Upton was playing with one of them, steering it by means of an electronic remote-control device which he held in one hand.

"Mr. Upton?" said Frank.

The bearded man turned to look at the two youths. "Hm, eh, yes. You must be Frank and Joe Hardy."

"Yes, sir. Let's get right to the point, if you don't mind."

"Whatever you say, son."

"First of all, we'd like to learn more about your relationship with Chelsea Builders. And then we want to know how soon we can talk to your son."

"Well, now, that's a fairly big order. Just what did you mean by that first question? Are you implying that Upton Associates or I may have something to do with that burglary you mentioned?"

114

Frank attempted to reply diplomatically. But Upton paid little attention. He seemed more interested in steering his toy boat across the water, and the Hardys had the odd impression that he was stalling for time.

Suddenly, as his boat reached the opposite side of the pond, they saw a young man stoop and snatch it up. Frank and Joe thought he slipped something into the little craft, but he acted so quickly and unexpectedly that neither could be sure.

As suddenly as he had picked up the boat, the youth put it back in the water. Then he turned and darted off among some trees.

Upton was already steering the boat back to their own side of the pond. As soon as it came within reach, he stooped down and plucked out a rolled-up slip of paper, which he handed to the Hardys.

"That young man you saw just now was my son Lew," he informed them.

Frank hastily unrolled the note. It bore a message scrawled in ink:

Mob job! Tell your father to watch out or we're both dead men!

14

The Mustached Stranger

The Hardy boys gasped as they read the strange warning that Lew Upton had sent them in the toy boat. Frank shot a puzzled glance at the bearded architect, who stood by watching them somberly.

"What's this all about, Mr. Upton?" he asked.

The man shrugged. "Don't ask me. I assumed you'd know. The message is meant for you."

He explained that, ever since getting out of prison a few weeks ago, his son had been living by himself, apparently somewhere in the city, but avoiding contact with his family.

"Lew said it was better that way for all of us, that he didn't want any of his underworld troubles brushing off on his mother and me," Zachary Upton went on.

"However, he would call us every so often, and he gave me a number where I could reach him in case of emergency. That's how I got in touch with him after you called today."

Upton related that his son had sounded very disturbed when he heard that the Hardys wanted to talk to him about the Chelsea Builders' burglary. "He told me that it was important to get a message to you fast, but he didn't want to be seen with any of us. That's why we arranged this toy boat gimmick."

Despite his gruff front, Upton was obviously very much worried about Lew's safety, especially in light of the first two words in the message. Mob job implied that some gangster setup was behind the safecracking.

Frank and Joe were also concerned about their father, although they knew he was usually well able to protect himself from criminals. But for the moment, neither the Hardy boys nor Zachary Upton could guess what had prompted the message.

The two young sleuths said good-by to the architect and retrieved their car from the parking garage. Soon they were heading homeward.

Arriving in Bayport, they learned that Fenton Hardy had not yet returned, so they decided to stay overnight before starting for the Adirondacks again.

"Maybe we'd better let Chet know our plans," Joe suggested.

"Good idea," said Frank and called the cottage. Before leaving Hawk River, the Hardys had cautioned

117

their stout chum to speak cagily over the phone for fear of their conversation being overheard by the gossipy local operator. Keeping this in mind, Chet managed to let Frank know by his remarks that he had kept a midnight vigil outside the Tabor house, but that nothing unusual had happened.

"Okay, Chet," Frank replied. "Same deal tonight. We'll see you tomorrow. We want to talk to Dad, so we're going to stick around in case he shows up this evening. Meanwhile, take care of yourself."

"You think I won't?"

Frank chuckled and hung up.

Before dinner, the boys drove to Wild World, an animal park outside Bayport. They asked their elderly friend, Pop Carter, who operated the establishment, if they could borrow a tranquilizer dart gun.

"We may need it to capture a werewolf, Pop," Frank explained.

"If anyone else had told me that," Pop replied, "I'd suspect that he was crazy. But with you Hardys I'm ready to believe anything!" He gave them the gun, and the brothers returned home.

By the following morning, there was still no word from their father. Hiding their own worried feelings, the boys did their best to reassure their mother and Aunt Gertrude. Soon they were on their way once more to the Adirondacks.

En route, the Hardys detoured to the Catskill Mountain area to visit the Pine Manor Rest Home. They asked at the reception desk if they could speak to the doctor who had treated John Tabor.

The receptionist smiled in surprise. "That's a coincidence!" she remarked. "Another visitor came in fifteen minutes ago asking the same thing. He's with Dr. Benton right now."

Frank and Joe sat down to await their turn, wondering who the visitor could be. When the receptionist finally escorted them down a hallway, they saw a man with a thick black mustache coming out of the doctor's office. The Hardys were curious if he was the person who had inquired about the young architect and his nervous breakdown.

Dr. Benton was a thin, fussy-looking individual. His manner seemed rather curt and impatient, as if he were tired of answering questions about the Tabor case. However, when the boys showed him the letter signed by his former patient, he agreed to spare them a few minutes.

"Do you mind telling us who that man was who just left here?" Frank asked.

"He came here for the same reason you did. It wouldn't be proper for me to discuss his business with you."

The physician told them briefly about the treatment which young Tabor had received at the sanatorium. He scoffed at any notion that his apparent breakdown might have been purely imaginary and brought on by outside enemies.

"That's ridiculous!" the doctor snapped. "John was definitely suffering from delusions. Even while he was here, he reported hearing the voices of his werewolf ancestors."

"They wouldn't be hard to fake," Joe pointed out. "With a few electronic gimmicks, we could make any patient here imagine the same thing."

Frank nodded. "That's true, sir. By hiding one or more miniaturized radio receivers in his room, we could be miles from the sanatorium and still broadcast such voices to a patient. By planting both a bug and a receiver, we could even make him think he was carrying on a two-way conversation with a ghost."

The doctor frowned. "To do that, you'd first have to get to his room. And I can assure you that none of John's so-called enemies had a chance to do that."

"A staff employee might have been bribed to plant the radio gimmicks," Joe reasoned.

"I resent any such suggestion, young man!"

"If you'll let us check the room John Tabor occupied while he was a patient here," Frank said, "we can soon tell you if it contains any bugs or other devices."

Dr. Benton seemed somewhat upset, but reluctantly agreed. The Hardys got a kit of detection gear which they had brought along in their car and proceeded to make an electronic sweep of the room in question. They not only checked the walls for hidden devices, but also the bedside lamp, furniture, and other items.

"No luck!" Joe grumbled.

"That doesn't prove the trickery didn't happen," Frank pointed out. "Whoever planted the gimmicks may have removed them as soon as John Tabor checked out of the sanatori—"

The older Hardy boy suddenly broke off speaking, shoved the chair he had been examining out of the way and darted toward the door.

"What's wrong?" Joe exclaimed.

"I saw a guy peeking at us!"

The two young sleuths rushed out in pursuit. As they emerged into the corridor, a door slammed shut down the hall. It appeared to lead to another wing of the sanatorium, but when the boys tried it, it would not open.

"He must've pushed the lock button as he went through!" Frank fumed.

"What did this eavesdropper look like?" Joe asked.

"I only got a brief glance at him. He was rather heavyset with light blond hair, dressed in white. Probably a male nurse or attendant."

"He could have been the guy who planted the radio gimmick!"

When Dr. Benton heard their story, he seemed more upset than ever. Instead of offering to help find the culprit, he insisted that the Hardys leave the sanatorium, pointing out that they had utterly failed to prove their suspicions.

The boys stopped at a roadside diner for sandwiches. Frank pulled out the name and address of the

owner of Eagle's Nest. "He lives near New Paltz, which isn't far from here," the boy stated. "Should we stop in and see him?"

"What have we got to lose?"

The client, whose name was Crawford, proved to be a wealthy retired businessman. A balding, courtly mannered old gentleman, he seemed delighted by the Hardys' visit.

"Come into my study, boys," he invited them. When they were comfortably seated, he said, "Now then, what can I do for you?"

Frank explained how they had happened to visit Eagle's Nest. Then he told about the gray-haired man in dark glasses who had eavesdropped on their conversation with Hank and later arranged to meet them at a restaurant in New York.

Mr. Crawford snapped his fingers. "I know exactly whom you're talking about!"

"Really, sir? We'd like to learn more about him. He called himself Mr. Nest, but Joe and I are certain that name is an alias."

"You bet it is! His real name is Marburg. He's an antique dealer who specializes in old manuscripts and autographs, or so he says."

"How did you meet him?" Joe asked.

"Well, shortly after I bought Eagle's Nest, there was a story in one of the New York papers. It reported that I was having the old mansion restored, how I planned to make it into a historic showplace. Next day I got a call from Marburg. He offered to buy any old documents that turned up during the restoration. I tried to be polite, *and* honest. Told him I didn't expect to find anything of value. After all, the house has been sitting up there in the woods for years, an empty shell just rotting away.

"But Marburg refused to take no for an answer. He kept pestering me with calls," Mr. Crawford went on. "Even drove all the way from New York City just to see me. Finally I became fed up. Didn't trust him, anyhow. He sounded like a crook to me. I told him I wanted nothing to do with him, and if he bothered me any more, I wouldn't even give him the chance to *bid* on anything that turned up."

"I wonder why he lied to us about his name," Frank mused.

"In my opinion," said the elderly businessman, "it merely confirms what I suspected all along. The man's dishonest. He's ready to go to any lengths to lay his hands on whatever valuable items come to light. But he recognized you as the Hardy boys. So he's trying to cover himself, hoping you won't be able to trace him if he has to resort to theft or trickery."

"What about the tomahawk he mentioned?" Joe asked. Mr. Crawford shrugged. "No telling. Wouldn't surprise me if it were part of some elaborate confidence game he's playing."

The Hardys thanked their elderly informant and resumed their drive to the Adirondacks. When they arrived at Hawk River in midafternoon, Chet burst out of the cabin to greet them.

"You really missed some action here last night!" he blurted.

Joe hopped out of the car and stretched his arms and legs. "What happened?"

"Plenty! For openers, there were more wolf howls and werewolf attacks."

"Were you keeping an eye on the Tabors' house?" Frank put in anxiously.

The chubby boy nodded and threw out his chest. "You bet I was. In fact I came near solving the mystery all by myself!"

"Well, don't keep us in suspense!" Joe urged. "Give us a blow-by-blow!"

"Okay, okay. If you'll listen and give me a chance, I will. I was up in the tree, same as before, see? Something seemed to be moving in the shadows, and all of a sudden I caught on. There was *another guy* keeping watch on the house!"

"Did you get a look at him, Chet?"

"Not right away. It was too dark where he was standing. As I told you, he was in the shadows. Let's just call him Mr. X."

"Suits us. But what happened?"

Chet related that shortly before midnight he had seen John Tabor sneak out of the house.

"Was this before or after the howls started?"

"Right after." The chubby youth shuddered. "Boy, it

was weird! Almost as if he heard the wild wolves calling him and was going out in the woods to join them! Anyway, Mr. X started tailing him. So naturally I followed both of them. And when they got out in the open more, out in the moonlight, I finally got a chance to see what Mr. X looked like. He was a thickset guy with a dark cap and a big droopy dark mustache."

The Hardys exclaimed almost in unison, "Same guy we saw at the sanatorium!"

Frank added more cautiously, "At least the description fits. Go on with your story, Chet."

Their stout chum reported that he had followed the two men up a wooded hillside. "We were going along quietly," he continued, "when suddenly I heard a twig crack, as if someone stepped on it. Not in front of me, *behind* me!"

Joe said, "Oh, oh, you mean someone was following *you?*"

"That's what it sounded like." Chet gulped as he recalled his feelings at that scary moment. "Man, I was really shook up!"

"What did you do?" Joe asked tensely.

"I froze for a moment, then crouched down in a clump of brush. I figured if somebody *was* shadowing me, I'd waylay him and grab him as he came by."

Frank waited for the climax of the story. "Any luck?"

"Oh, I caught him all right," Chet said ruefully. "But I'm not sure how lucky I was. The guy fought like a wildcat. We were rolling all around in the dark, then he grabbed a stone and conked me on the head. When I came to everything was silent. So I came back here to the cabin. And I never even got a good look at the fellow I was scrapping with!"

"Never mind. You did fine, Chet, and showed plenty of nerve in a tight spot." Frank clapped the boy on the back, then frowned thoughtfully. "But this gives the case a new twist. Two other guys keeping John Tabor under surveillance!"

"Any hunches about who they are?" Joe asked, eyeing his brother hopefully.

"No. But I'd sure like to know where John was going. Could you show us the route he took, Chet?"

Chet Morton shrugged. "I could try."

The three boys drove to a spot near the Tabor house, then parked and got out, with Chet leading the way. He guided them away from the road, through a ragged patch of woods and over a rough, uneven stretch of terrain. Finally, they clambered up a hillside.

"Hey, look!" Joe exclaimed, pointing ahead.

Beyond the trees, they glimpsed a small hut.

"Wow! I didn't see that last night!" said Chet. "That must be where John Tabor was heading!"

The Bayport trio pressed forward and entered the hut. It was littered with books and papers. Besides a table, chair, cot, and wood stove, there was a drawing board with an architectural sketch pinned to it, and various drafting instruments. Electricity was supplied by a small generator.

"This must be where John comes to study and sketch out ideas for his designs," said Frank, glancing around with interest.

"Hey! Look at this!" Joe said, holding up what appeared to be a fur rug.

"It's a wolf skin!" gasped Chet.

"Right! Complete from nose to tail. The head even has glass eyes!"

Frank, who hurried to his brother's side, turned it over. "And leather straps with buckles are on the underside, so a person can strap it on!"

In their excitement over the find, the boys failed to hear footsteps approaching outside the hut. Suddenly the door burst open and a voice bellowed:

"You're all under arrest!"

15

Paleface Archer

The boys whirled to face the speaker. He was a tall, rawboned man wearing a stetson felt hat and a sheriff's badge pinned to the olive-gray jacket of his uniform.

"Under arrest for what?" Frank asked.

"Breaking and entering'll do for a start."

"We didn't break in, Sheriff. The door was open." Frank identified himself and his brother, as well as Chet, and explained that they were investigating the werewolf mystery.

On hearing that two of the youths were the sons of the famous detective, Fenton Hardy, the lawman relaxed his angry expression somewhat and even shook hands. "I'm Sheriff Kennig," he told them. "You can forget what I said about being under arrest. But that still doesn't excuse you for poking around without permission. I'm the local law officer. If you're up here to work on a case, you should've checked in with me first."

The Hardys thought it best not to argue.

"We're still fairly new at detective work, Sheriff. We don't have your experience at crime-fighting," Frank said diplomatically. "I guess we have a few things to learn."

The rawboned police officer seemed mollified by Frank's attitude and shrugged a bit pompously. "We all have to start somewhere," he said. "What's that you're holding, young fellow?"

"A wolf skin," Joe said, handing it over.

"Hm." Kennig examined the hide, obviously mystified but doing his best to look professional. "I'll take charge of this. It may be important evidence."

"How did you know we were here, Sheriff?" Joe inquired.

"I didn't. Just got a phone tip that it might be worthwhile to take a look in John Tabor's cabin." He added, "As your Dad may have told you, that's one of the most important techniques in police work—gathering leads from informers."

"Any idea who the caller was?" Frank asked.

Sheriff Kennig cleared his throat. "Actually, no. He didn't leave any name. But he spoke with a foreign accent."

The lawman fished a gleaming metal pellet from his

jacket pocket and held it out to show the boys. "Here's something else that may interest you fellows, strictly off the record, you understand."

"A silver bullet!" Joe exclaimed. "Where'd it come from, Sheriff?"

"When that werewolf was prowling around last night, someone took a shot at it. I dug this out of the bark of the tree where it hit. Didn't get too mashed up."

Chet started to say something. Frank sensed that he might be about to mention the bullet fired into the Hardys' front door in Bayport, which might have led to lengthy questioning by the sheriff. So he silenced his chum with a quick frown. Instead, Chet said, "Er, silver bullets are what people used to say it took to kill a werewolf, right?"

The sheriff nodded. "Uh-huh. And this isn't the only one that turned up."

Frank flashed him a startled glance. "Where else?"

"Somebody fired one at Karel Tabor this morning. Happened just as he was climbing into his helicopter to take off for New York."

"Did anyone spot the gunman?"

"Nope. The shot came from the woods near the Tabor's house. Whoever it was, looks as if someone around Hawk River may figure the best way to get rid of werewolves is to wipe out the Tabor family!"

"After telling the sheriff where they could be reached, the Hardys headed back to their car with Chet. Both Frank and Joe were worried that the furry clue they had discovered in the hut might cause fresh trouble for the Tabors.

"You think the sheriff would go as far as tossing John in the clink?" Chet asked owlishly.

"He just might," Frank replied, "if people around here get worked up enough about the werewolf attacks."

"I still don't see how anyone could be deceived by that wolf skin , though," Joe argued. "Even if someone strapped it to his arms and body, I wouldn't be fooled into thinking it was a real werewolf!"

"Neither would I," Chet chimed in.

"And it sure wouldn't explain that glowing wolf creature we saw at the Bayport Diner," Frank pointed out.

Suddenly Joe snapped his fingers. "Hey! I'll bet I know where that pelt came from!"

"Where?"

"Off that stuffed wolf that got stolen from Alec Virgil! That would explain the glass eyes!"

"Right," his brother agreed. "Someone just emptied out the stuffing. I think you've hit it, Joe."

Frank was thoughtful when they arrived at the cottage. "Do you suppose the Mohawks knew anything about werewolves?" he mused.

"Sure," Joe replied. "That book by Desmond Quorn says that American Indian tribes had lots of folktales about people turning into animals. Why?"

"Hank Eagle said his uncle's a medicine man, remember? Just for the fun of it, I'd like to hear what *he* has to say about this werewolf scare. Who knows, he might come up with some kind of Indian lore or wolf-hunting gimmick that we could use to distract people around here and take some of the heat off the Tabors." Frank looked at his two companions. "Are you game to drive to Hank's village?"

Joe nodded, and Chet was positively enthusiastic about the idea. A visit with the Indians, he felt, would give him a chance to soak up some real wilderness know-how. When the trio set off in the car again a short time later, the stout youth was clad in his fringed buckskin hunting shirt and headband, and even brought along his bow and arrows.

The Mohawk village, as they found out by asking directions, lay only a few miles from Hawk River. To Chet's disappointment, it consisted only of a few weatherbeaten houses and cabins, and the people, aside from their coppery complexions and, in some cases, braided hair, seemed no different from other local Americans.

"Chet looks more Indian than they do," Joe remarked with a chuckle to Frank.

The Mohawks seemed to think so, too. When the boys climbed out of the car, a group of children who had been playing in front of the general store immediately surrounded the chubby visitor, admiring his bow and arrows and asking questions about his costume.

Meantime, Frank and Joe asked where Hank Eagle's

uncle lived. His name was Adam Eagle, and he proved to be a thin, gnarled-looking old man with a beaky nose and high-cheekboned face. When he heard that his callers were friends of his nephew he greeted them with a firm handshake.

"*Say-go! Skaw-non-gowa,* my friends. How are you?"

The boys chatted with him and found out that Adam Eagle, too, had been a high-steeler in his youth. He had helped build the George Washington Bridge across the Hudson River and the Empire State Building, but now worked as a carpenter and odd-job man.

"Hank told us you were a medicine man," Joe remarked.

The elderly Mohawk shrugged. "Sometimes I make herbal remedies for my neighbors when they are ill, and perform tribal ceremonies."

It turned out that he had already heard about the werewolf attacks at Hawk River. When Frank asked his opinion about them and how the trouble could be stopped, at first Mr. Eagle would say little.

But finally, as a favor to the boys, he donned an Indian costume and built a small fire of twigs in the fireplace of his cabin. He played eerily on a red cedar flute. Then, shaking a pair of gourd rattles and speaking in the Mohawk tongue, he began calling on *Ga-oh,* the Spirit of the Winds. Frank and Joe got goose pimples listening to the weird chant.

Afterward, the old man said to them, "The woods are

134

full of mystery, my friends. Most people have lost touch with nature. Who can say whether or not men may become like animals? Still, I think the trouble you speak of comes not from any wolf. I see you in the fire, hunting down evil persons!"

Somewhat mystified but impressed, the Hardys thanked the medicine man and went out to look for Chet. They found him showing off his skill at archery, taking turns with some of the village teenagers, shooting arrows at a makeshift target. The Indian youths clapped when he managed to hit the bull's-eye every time.

But none of the Bayporters could match the Mohawks when it came to hurling a hickory lance at a rolling ring. Later they played the deer-button game. The buttons, made of polished horn, were each charred on one side. The players shook the buttons in one hand like dice, then threw them on a blanket, trying to make six or more buttons land with the same side turned up.

Much to his delight, Chet won more games than anyone else. He and the Hardys were invited by the villagers to stay for supper. It was a feast of corn soup, fried trout, venison, succotash, squash, cornbread and blueberry pie.

Before the visitors left, some of the village girls presented Chet with a beaded headband they had sewed, as a prize for his marksmanship with bow and arrow.

"*Ohna-ghee-wahee!*" the Mohawks called, waving good-by.

Chet was so proud of the trophy he wanted to show it off to Alena. He asked the Hardys to stop by the Tabors' house when they returned to Hawk River. However, when it came to ringing the bell, he seemed a bit nervous.

"What's the matter?" Frank asked. "Feeling shy?"

"That goofy housekeeper doesn't like me," Chet confessed sheepishly as he got out of the car. "What if *she* answers the door?"

Dusk had fallen and the boys saw Alena pass in front of a lighted window. Then the light went out.

Chet had a sudden inspiration. He wrote a note to Alena, tied it to an arrow, and strode halfway up the drive while Frank and Joe waited in the car. He aimed at Alena's still open window and let the arrow fly.

Unfortunately, his nervousness must have spoiled his aim. There was a loud tinkle of glass, and Chet froze in horror. His arrow had crashed into the wrong window!

Next moment the front door burst open and Pocahontas charged out, bellowing and brandishing a broom!

16

Tomahawk Reward

"Clear outa here, you no-good!" the huge housekeeper roared, shaking her broomstick weapon. "I'll teach you to come breaking windows in this house!"

Chet pounded down the drive in panic as fast as his chubby legs could carry him. "Gun the engine!" he shouted while still ten yards from the car.

"How come?" teased Joe, who was at the wheel. "Don't you want to stick around till Alena reads your note?"

"Never mind the wisecracks, just get going!" Chet leaped aboard, bug-eyed and puffing. "Think I want that giantess to brain me with her war club?"

Once back in the safety of their cottage, the stout youth began stoking up on cocoa and doughnuts.

"Having someone like Pocahontas chase after him is hard on a guy's nerves," he said plaintively. "I have to recharge my batteries!"

"Good idea," said Frank. "We may need your full power tonight."

"What for?" Chet blurted, eyeing the Hardy boy suspiciously.

"All three of us are going to stake out the Tabors' house. If any of those guys who were out there last night show up again, we'll nab them!"

Around nine-thirty, just as the boys were about to leave the cabin, the phone rang. Joe answered. The caller was Hank Eagle.

"I just got home from New York," the Mohawk high-steeler said. "My uncle told me you were here at the village this afternoon. Sorry I missed you."

"Same here," Joe said. "But we sure enjoyed the visit. Your uncle's a fine man, Hank."

"He thinks you Hardys are pretty special, too. When he 'made medicine' over the fire, he says *Ga-oh* told him you could be trusted, so he advised me to tell you the truth."

"About what?"

"About that sneaky dude you met in the restaurant, the one who called himself Mr. Nest. His real name is Marburg."

"We already found that out," Joe said. "But if you've got something more to tell us, wait till I get Frank on the line, so he can hear it, too!"

138

The Hardys were fascinated as they listened to the story Hank Eagle related. After the Revolutionary War, his ancestor, Dark Eagle, had sailed on a British troopship, carrying redcoats home to England. In London, King George had presented his fierce Indian ally with a silver tomahawk in reward for his services to the Crown. Made by a famous English silversmith, the tomahawk was decorated with a gold design and embossed with several diamonds.

"Wow! What happened to it?" Joe exclaimed.

"Nobody knows," Hank replied. "Remember, that was two hundred years ago. Somehow, the tomahawk got lost or disappeared from sight during those two centuries. But when you told me what Marburg said in the restaurant, I knew right away that's what he was after."

Frank said, "How would he know about the tomahawk?"

"From history books. It's no secret. Anyone who's interested in antiques could have heard about it."

Hank went on to tell that his family possessed an old journal or diary kept by Dark Eagle. "Many pages are too faded and moldy to read, but from various legible remarks, I'm sure the tomahawk is hidden somewhere at Eagle's Nest."

"Would Marburg know about that diary, too?" Joe asked.

"Probably. We've tried our best to keep it secret; in fact, it's stored in a safe deposit box. But several historians know Dark Eagle kept such a diary, so the news may easily have leaked out to Marburg."

Hank said he became more and more convinced of this when Marburg came to see him and tried to work his way into the Mohawk's confidence. "Then when he saw you guys talking to me and recognized you from news pictures as the sons of Fenton Hardy, he probably figured you were after the same prize he was."

Frank told the high-steeler about the chat he and Joe had had with Mr. Crawford, and added, "Probably Marburg figured if you didn't have the diary, it might just turn up when the old mansion is restored."

"Quite likely," Hank agreed, "and he's hoping if he can lay hands on it that the diary will clue him in to what happened to the tomahawk."

The Hardys thanked the construction worker for telling them his family's secret. They also promised to let him know if they gleaned any clues to the whereabouts of the tomahawk. Then they set off with Chet for the Tabor estate.

Parking their car out of sight, the boys chose a different tree from the one Chet had used for his lookout post. All three found places to perch themselves in its sturdy branches. In the moonlight, they could see the house clearly.

Less than half an hour later, Joe hissed a soft warning and pointed to the left. A stealthy figure had just emerged from among the trees and was moving closer to the house.

140

"You stay here, Chet," Frank whispered, "and keep your eyes peeled for any other intruders. Joe and I'll go get this guy, okay?"

"Check!" their stout chum agreed.

Letting themselves down from the tree, the Hardys closed in fast and silently on their quarry. He had taken up a position in a clump of shrubbery, which gave him a view of both the patio and the front of the house.

But he was unprepared for an assault from behind. Before he realized what was happening, Frank hooked an arm around his windpipe and clamped a hand over his mouth. Joe grabbed the man's wrist and twisted it painfully behind him.

Between them, they marched him well out of earshot of the house. He was the mustached man whom they had seen leaving Dr. Benton's office at the Pine Manor Rest Home!

"Suppose you tell us what you're doing here, spying on the Tabors," Frank said.

"Why should I tell you anything?" the prisoner retorted.

"Because if you don't we'll call Sheriff Kennig and you can try explaining to him!" Joe warned.

The mustached man scowled and hesitated, then shrugged. "Okay, you win. My name's Elmo Yancey. I'm a private eye."

"Prove it," snapped Frank.

The man pulled a billfold from his inside coat pocket. He opened it and presented them with his private investigator's license for the State of New York. The Hardys inspected it, and Frank nodded. "Good enough."

Yancey said he had been hired by a client to investigate and report on the Tabor family, especially the son. After coming to Hawk River, he heard about the werewolf who was said to be haunting the area. Then he read the news story hinting that John Tabor might be the culprit due to a family taint. Next day an unsigned note came to his motel in the mail, informing him that the young architect had been a mental patient at the Pine Manor Rest Home. So he went there to try to interview John's doctor.

"What about last night? And don't hand us any baloney," Frank added. "You were under surveillance."

"Then why ask?"

"We want to hear your version. It's one way to find out if you're leveling with us."

Yancey said he had decided to keep watch on the Tabor house to see if John slipped out after dark and had anything to do with the werewolf attacks. "He showed, all right, and he was acting pretty odd."

"How do you mean?" Joe said.

"He was moving like a sleepwalker, almost as if he were in a trance. I followed him for a while. He headed up a hillside, a little way north of here. I lost sight of him for a moment or two, but then I saw a gleam of light appear up near the top of the hill."

Frank frowned on hearing this. Chet had made no mention of any light. However, Frank reflected that it might not have been visible from their chum's position farther down the hillside.

"Right after that," Yancey went on, "I heard a scuffle break out somewhere below me. John Tabor must've heard it too, because the light went out, and then I caught sight of him again."

Yancey said that the young architect had headed homeward by a different route. The investigator himself had followed in order to make sure of where John was going. Afterward, Yancey had returned to the hillside to check on the scene of the scuffle, but found no one there. He had then discovered the hut near the top of the hill, from where the light had come.

"You looked inside?" Frank inquired.

"Naturally. It wasn't locked."

"Did you see a wolf skin in there?"

The private eye seemed startled by the question, but shook his head. "Nope, just books and architectural drawing gear. It looked as if John had used the place as a private studio where he could go off to study or work on plans."

"You're sure there was no fur pelt lying around?" Joe persisted.

"Positive. If there'd been anything like that, you can bet I'd have spotted it."

The Hardys exchanged glances. If Yancey's testimony was true, then the wolf skin must have been planted in the hut later, maybe by the same person who had tipped off the sheriff!

"How come you're back tonight?" Frank inquired.

Yancey shrugged. "I didn't really learn anything last evening. I figured tonight I might be luckier. But it sure didn't turn out that way," he added ruefully.

"Who is your client?" the older Hardy asked abruptly, hoping he might catch the detective off guard.

"You don't expect me to answer that, do you? No ethical private investigator reveals his client's identity without permission."

"We understand." Frank grinned and introduced himself and Joe.

Elmo Yancey's attitude changed immediately on learning that they were the sons of Fenton Hardy. He promised to tell them his client's name if and when he was allowed to do so. Meanwhile, he stayed with the Hardys and Chet, keeping watch on the Tabor's house. But when nothing happened by midnight, he abandoned his vigil.

The Bayport trio maintained their stakeout an hour longer. Then they, too, gave up for the night.

Next morning, Frank and Joe were relieved to get a radio call from their father. They filled him in on all that had happened, both in New York and in Hawk River.

Fenton Hardy, in turn, revealed that Bubbles Upton,

144

the son of the burly architect, was now working on the side of the law, trying to make up for the crime that had led to his jail sentence and thus redeem himself in the eyes of the authorities.

"Is he helping you on this case, Dad?" Joe inquired.

"Yes, he's checking out the possibility that a crooked contractor may be mixed up in those building disasters."

"Same angle Neal Xavier mentioned to us?"

"Right. But now I want you fellows to check out a brand-new lead for me in New York City. It may be urgent, so I'm sending Jack Wayne to fly you there."

The detective gave his sons careful instructions and on Chet's request, agreed that their stout chum could go with them.

"One other thing, Dad," put in Frank. "Could you give us the name of a psychiatrist in New York that we could talk to while we're there? I'd like to get another opinion on John Tabor's behavior."

"Good idea," said Fenton Hardy. He named a reliable expert whom he himself had consulted in connection with various criminal cases.

"Thanks, Dad, and watch yourself. Remember the warning note Bubbles sent to us in Central Park."

"Right, son, and you do the same. This assignment could be dangerous."

Jack Wayne often flew Mr. Hardy's private plane, *Skyhappy Sal*. An hour after the detective's call, the small craft landed at an airfield near Hawk River. The

145

boys greeted the friendly pilot, then all set off for LaGuardia Airport in New York.

From there they taxied to the address Fenton Hardy had given them in a slummy area of the Bronx. It was a narrow-fronted, two-story brownstone house, squeezed between half-ruined tenement buildings. The boys scouted the scene first, then rang the bell. No one answered.

"Door's open," Joe noted. "Let's go in."

Frank led the way cautiously, through a dirty, tiled vestibule into the first-floor living room. All three gasped at the sight of a motionless figure lying bound and gagged on the floor.

"It's Bubbles Upton!" Joe exclaimed.

Chet blurted in dismay, "He's dead!"

17

The Flying Chicken

Frank rushed across the room, with his two companions close behind, and they examined the man on the floor. It was apparent from his bruised face and torn, red-stained clothes that young Upton had been badly beaten. But he was still breathing, and Frank was able to detect a fairly strong pulse.

"He'll be okay, if we get him to a doctor," the older Hardy boy declared. "Help me untie him."

He took off Bubbles' gag while Joe and Chet removed the rope from the young man's wrists and ankles. Then they lifted him onto a sofa.

Joe hurried into the kitchen to fetch a glass of water. A few swallows were forced between the victim's lips as Frank chafed his wrists. Soon young Upton opened his eyes.

"H—how did you guys get here?" he asked weakly.

"My father sent us," Frank informed him.

"Thank goodness. Then he—he must have clued in to my code signal." Bubbles explained that he had paid a ham radio operator to broadcast a call when he could not reach Fenton Hardy by phone.

Joe said, "Feel strong enough to tell us what happened?"

"I'll t—try," Bubbles responded. He said he had been hired by mobsters to crack the Chelsea Builders safe. "And I'm sure those same crooks who hired me are in cahoots with the contractor your father's investigating!"

"What did they want out of the safe?" Frank asked.

"Some sound tapes."

A look flashed between the Hardys. Once again Neal Xavier's charges seemed to be confirmed by outside testimony!

"Do you know what was on them?" Frank pursued.

Bubbles shook his head painfully. "No. I tried to play them to find out, but the mobsters caught me and beat me up. They planned to dump me in the river after dark."

Both Hardys wondered if young Upton realized the tapes might incriminate his own father. But they decided not to risk upsetting him while he was in such condition.

"We'll call an ambulance and get you to a hospital pronto!" Frank promised, looking around for a telephone.

148

But Bubbles insisted that it would be safer all around if the Hardys stayed out of the picture completely, so that no one could connect him with them or their father. "Besides, I'm not in bad enough shape to need an ambulance," he gasped hoarsely. "A taxi will do."

He protested so anxiously that the Hardys gave in. Joe hurried to the nearby corner and flagged a cruising cab. Bubbles Upton was helped into it, and the driver instructed to take him to the closest hospital.

The three Bayporters then proceeded by subway to the office of the psychiatrist that Fenton Hardy had recommended. The receptionist told them that the detective had already phoned for an emergency appointment, and after a short wait, they were waved into the doctor's consulting room.

Dr. Fizzoli, a bespectacled man with thick, dark hair fringing his bald head, asked the boys how he could help them.

Frank described John Tabor's weird behavior. "Is there any way a person could be influenced to do such things?" he went on, "and then not even remember what happened?"

"Of course," the doctor nodded. "Almost anyone could be made to behave that way, by post-hypnotic suggestion."

To accomplish this, he explained the person would first be hypnotized, then given an order to carry out after he woke up from his trance, perhaps quite a while afterward.

149

"The more often a person is hypnotized," Dr. Fizzoli went on, "the easier it comes to control him. Yet, when he's snapped out of his trance, he may not even remember being given any orders."

"Would he recall carrying them out?" Frank asked.

"Not if he'd been programmed to forget them."

Joe said, "But how would he know *when* to carry out the order?"

"Usually, the programming involves some sort of signal," replied the doctor. "For instance, the hypnotist may say, 'When you see me scratch my ear, you will do so and so.' And later on, after the patient's been brought out of his trance, the hypnotist scratches his ear and the patient does exactly what he was told to do."

With a smile, Dr. Fizzoli added, "If you ask him *why* he did such a thing, he'll make up all sorts of reasons. It never seems to occur to him that he may be carrying out a post-hypnotic suggestion."

Suddenly Frank remembered how John had been called to the phone during the barbecue party. A little later, when he came out of the house again, he had acted like a zombie.

"How about a signal over the phone?" he inquired. "Would that work?"

"Perfectly," said Dr. Fizzoli. "In fact, the phone voice, if it *is* a voice, could be used to reinforce or strengthen the original command. But the signal could just as easily be a buzzer or a handclap or a certain bit of music, whatever."

150

"What if the person didn't *want* to carry out the command?"

"Once he's been hypnotized, he has no choice."

Chet had been listening with a skeptical expression. "Hm, maybe some people are like that," he scoffed, "but I'd like to see somebody make *me* do something I didn't want to do!"

Dr. Fizzoli smiled. "Shall we try?"

"Go ahead," Chet challenged him.

The doctor held up a shiny coin on the end of a chain. He asked the chubby youth to gaze at it as it swung to and fro. Then, in a monotonous voice, he began to suggest that Chet was feeling relaxed and drowsy, that his limbs were growing heavier and losing all feeling, and finally that Chet would do whatever he was told.

Chet carried out several simple commands, such as shivering as if he were cold, barking like a dog, and dancing around the room. But later, after the doctor snapped his fingers to bring him out of his trance, Chet insisted he had never even been *in* a trance.

"I was wide awake all along. I knew what was going on. When you asked me to do something, I cooperated, but I didn't have to do it."

The doctor shrugged and smiled. "Perhaps so. Many subjects feel that way. The fact remains that you did what I told you to."

The Hardys grinned and thanked Dr. Fizzoli for his information and demonstration. Before leaving the office, Frank asked the receptionist if he might use her phone.

"Of course," she said. "Let me get you an outside line first, then just dial the number."

Frank had Jack Wayne paged at LaGuardia Airport. When the pilot answered, the young detective told him to start warming up *Skyhappy Sal*. The boys would be ready for takeoff as soon as they taxied to the airfield.

"Maybe not as soon as you think " Jack replied. He said that an urgent message had been relayed from Bayport.

"From whom?" Frank asked.

"Some guy employed by Chelsea Builders, named Neal Xavier. He phoned your home, your aunt broadcast his message, and I picked it up on the radio."

"What does he want?"

"To see you and Joe as soon as possible. He says it's very important, but the meeting must be kept secret. You're to come to his apartment on Central Park West instead of the company office."

The boys were soon on their way by taxi to Xavier's address.

"Who is this guy?" Chet asked en route.

"Karel Tabor's executive assistant," Joe told him.

When they arrived at his apartment, the trio were surprised to find themselves facing a big, powerful, snarling Doberman guard dog held on a tight leash by Neal Xavier, who seemed tense and frightened.

"I rented him from a trainer last night for pro-

152

tection," Xavier told the boys. "Sit down, please, and I'll explain."

Pacing nervously back and forth while his dog sat watchfully eyeing the three visitors, Xavier began, "I've made a very unpleasant discovery. Much as I hate to say so, I now believe that the real criminal behind the firm's troubles is none other than my boss—Karel Tabor!"

The Bayporters were shocked by the news.

"What makes you think so?" Joe asked keenly.

Xavier explained that Tabor, despite his brilliant reputation, had long been at odds with Chelsea Builders' board of directors. He had, therefore, deliberately arranged the three building disasters which Mr. Hardy was investigating, in order to force down the price of Chelsea Builders' stock.

Frank frowned. "Why would he want to do that?"

"So he can buy it up cheaply and gain control of the company."

"How did he arrange the disasters?" Joe asked.

"Through that crooked contractor I mentioned. All three were due to sabotage carried out by mobsters. He told me those tapes contained evidence linking the contractor with Upton Associates. But now I'm sure they implicated Tabor himself. He was keeping them as insurance, to make sure the contractor didn't double-cross him."

"How did you find all this out?" Frank inquired.

"Just a lucky break, if you can call it lucky." Xavier

154

explained that, by chance, he had overheard a phone conversation between Tabor and the contractor. "They were setting up a meeting at ten o'clock tonight, at a house near Hawk River. If they get wise that I was listening in, my life won't be worth a plugged nickel!"

After learning the cabin's location, the boys taxied to LaGuardia and flew back to the Adirondacks. Frank and Joe had left their car parked at the airfield near Hawk River. On landing, they drove to the cabin.

Frank braked to a stop and said, "Well, here we are!"

Chet immediately leaped out of the car, flapping his arms. "Look! I'm a chicken!" he cried, cackling loudly. "I can fly!"

"Good for you!" said a girl's voice. "May I watch you take off?"

Chet whirled and saw Alena Tabor walking toward them!

18

Nine O'Clock Shadow

Chet's face blushed fiery red with embarrassment when he suddenly realized what he was doing. The Hardys burst out laughing.

"Good grief!" Chet moaned. "Whatever made me do such a goofy thing?"

"A post-hypnotic suggestion, that's what!" said Joe.

"Huh?"

"You were just doing what you were told to do," Frank added.

Chet stared at the Hardys, his cheeks still flaming. "What're you guys talking about?"

Frank explained that, while under hypnosis in the psychiatrist's office, Dr. Fizzoli had ordered their chum to act like a flying chicken when they arrived at their cabin.

"Cheer up, Chet." Joe chuckled. "He only did it to convince you such things are possible. Frank signaled you when he said, 'Well here we are!'"

To save Chet further embarrassment, Frank turned to their visitor. "What's up, Alena?"

Her face fell after her momentary amusement. "Oh, I'm so worried about John!" she replied. "Sheriff Kennig's been grilling him all afternoon. He's even warned him not to leave Hawk River. Dad and I are afraid he may soon be arrested!"

"Well, you can stop worrying," Frank told her. "I think we've just found out what makes your brother take those midnight strolls."

"What do you mean?" Alena exclaimed, her eyes widening in surprise.

Frank reported what they had learned from the psychiatrist about post-hypnotic suggestion, and went on, "I'm convinced something like that must have happened to John. Someone has hypnotized him deeply and ordered him to leave the house in the middle of the night. Do you remember whether he got a late phone call just before bedtime on Wednesday night?"

"Yes, as a matter of fact, he did. Why?"

"Same thing happened the night of the barbecue. Those calls may be from the person who hypnotized him, to give him reinforcing suggestions. Later, a wolf howl outside, even if it's a fake howl, is the signal that prompts him to leave the house."

157

"It would also explain why he acts like he's in a trance," said Joe. "Chet's just demonstrated to you how the whole thing works."

The plump girl's face broke into a happy smile. "Oh, that's wonderful!" she gushed. "You've no idea how relieved Dad will be when I tell him! Thank you all so very much!"

Before Chet realized what was happening, Alena flung her arms around his neck and kissed him a resounding smack on the cheek.

The chubby Bayporter's cheeks turned flaming pink again, but this time with bashful pleasure rather than embarrassment.

Meanwhile, Frank and Joe exchanged hasty glances of amusement mixed with concern. Both were thinking the same thing, that they had better not tell Alena about Neal Xavier's accusation against her father, and thus spoil her happiness of the moment. She drove off in her red miniwagon soon afterward, eager to tell her father the good news.

Later, as the boys were finishing supper, they heard a knock. Frank got up to answer the door. Their visitor proved to be Elmo Yancey.

"Come on in!" Frank said. "You're just in time for a cup of coffee."

"Thanks. Don't mind if I do." The private eye joined them at the table and proceeded to tell the news that had brought him to their cabin. "I just got a cablegram over the phone from my client. It's in reply to one I sent him this morning, and it gives me permission to use my judgment about telling you his name. But the information must be kept in strict confidence, of course."

"We understand," Frank assured him. "You can count on us to keep our lips zipped."

"Who is he?" Joe asked eagerly.

"A wealthy European businessman who lives in Paris. His name is Gustav Tabor."

"Tabor?" Joe echoed, and shot a glance at Frank. "That must be the distant cousin Mr. Tabor mentioned to us, the one who escaped to the West just before Czechoslovakia went Communist."

"Right," Frank agreed, and turned to Elmo Yancey. "How come he hired you to report on the American branch of the family?"

"Because he's old and rich and looking for an heir. He has no children of his own, so he's decided to leave his fortune to the youngest male Tabor over here. But first he wants a character check on both John and his father, Karel Tabor, to see if John is worthy of inheriting."

Chet whistled and murmured, "Well, what do you know!"

The Hardys thanked Yancey for the information. Later, after he had gone, Joe said to his brother, "You realize this may explain the whole werewolf business?"

Frank nodded thoughtfully. "I'll say I do! It could mean someone's deliberately trying to smear John and ruin his chances of inheriting Gustav Tabor's fortune."

159

"Right! But who?" Joe mused.

"You want a suggestion?"

"Let's hear it."

"How about the Frenchman who called on Desmond Quorn for information about the Tabor family werewolves?"

"Hey! You're right!" Joe exclaimed, socking his fist into his palm. "Then he steals the file and mails it, along with a copy of the magazine article, to the editor of the local newspaper, just to make sure everyone gets the message that John's slightly nutty and gets wolfman delusions every full moon!"

"Which wouldn't help John's chances of becoming Gustav Tabor's heir," Frank agreed.

"And to put him even deeper into the soup," Joe went on, "the Frenchman gets hold of a wolf skin and plants it in John's studio hut."

"Just two things wrong with your theory," Frank mused.

"What?" spoke up Chet, who was munching doughnuts and listening to the Hardys' conversation with great interest.

"One, it doesn't explain the glowing wolf-creature."

Joe cocked a quizzical eyebrow. "And two?"

"Even if we're right," said Frank, "why is the culprit doing it, and how do we find him? We don't know a thing about him."

"Wrong," said Chet, between mouthfuls of pastry. "You know at least *one* thing about him."

160

"Name it," Frank said.

"He said his name was Julien Sorel."

"So what?" Joe shrugged. "It's not likely he'd use his real name."

Frank puckered his forehead. "Probably not. But Chet may have a point there. That name might just mean something to a member of the Tabor family."

"Hm, could be. Let's give it a whirl." Picking up the telephone, Joe called the Tabors' number. Alena answered. After telling her who he was, Joe said, "Does the name 'Julien Sorel' mean anything to you, Alena?"

"Of course!"

"Who is he?"

"The hero of a famous French novel by Stendhal, called *The Red and the Black*."

Joe groaned. "Thanks anyhow, Alena, but forget I asked."

Shortly before nine o'clock, the Hardys set out by car for the house where Karel Tabor was to meet the crooked contractor. Xavier had told the boys its exact location, which he had overheard while eavesdropping on the plotters' telephone conversation. The Hardys hoped to arrive in time to stake out the place before the meeting took place. Meanwhile, they left Chet to hold the fort and keep watch on the Tabors' house.

Frank was at the wheel as they tooled along the forest-fringed highway in the moonlight. "Don't look now, Joe," he murmured, "but I think we're being tailed."

"Lights in the rearview mirror?"

"No. Its headlights are out. That's what worries me, but I can see the car fairly well as long as the moon doesn't go behind a cloud. Whoever it is, he's been keeping the same distance behind us for almost ten miles."

Joe proposed a plan which Frank thought might work although it had possible dangers. The older Hardy slowed his speed somewhat, keeping an eye peeled for any turnoffs.

Presently he wheeled right onto a rutted lane which wound among a stand of oaks and evergreens, interspersed with clumps of underbrush. The growth was dense enough to screen the glow of their headlights from the highway.

Soon Frank veered again, swinging the car off the lane and into the first narrow space among the trees that presented itself. Then he switched off their lights and the boys waited.

In a few minutes the tail car came along the lane in cautious pursuit. Its driver had been forced to turn on his parking lights to see his way ahead.

No sooner had the car gone by than Frank vroomed his engine and backed out of their parking space, blocking the lane. As he switched on his lights, they saw the tail car slow to a halt, almost, it seemed, with an audible groan of despair. Its driver obviously realized that he was trapped. To keep going would have meant the risk of getting lost or disabled in the back country wilderness at night, well off the main artery.

It seemed simpler to give up the game as Joe and Frank gambled it would. There was a minute or two of silence. Then they saw the door of the tail car open. The driver got out in the glare of their headlights, with his hands up in a gesture of surrender. He was a young man in his twenties with wavy brown hair. His clothes seemed of foreign cut.

The Hardys stayed in their seats, letting the stranger approach the front of their car. Then Frank switched on his high beams, dazzling the stranger still more. If he thought they had him covered with a gun, so much the better.

"Don't come any closer," Frank growled. "Just toss us your identification and you won't get hurt."

The stranger threw what looked like a thin, leather-bound booklet. Frank caught it. It was a French passport in the name of Paul Clermont. Then came a letter of introduction in English from a bank in Paris.

"Oh, oh," Joe muttered as the Hardys glanced over the letter. It mentioned that the bearer, Paul Clermont, was a brother-in-law of the well-known financier, Gustav Tabor.

Frank turned down his high beams, and the boys got out to confront the Frenchman. Realizing the two young sleuths had him cornered, Clermont glumly admitted what they had already guessed. Namely, that he was attempting to spoil John's chances of inheriting Gustav Tabor's fortune by making the young architect seem like a dangerous lunatic.

"But surely that is no great crime," Clermont insisted. "The worst you can call it is a cruel prank."

"A prank to cheat John out of his rightful inheritance!" Frank retorted.

"You also stole a folder from Desmond Quorn's files," Joe added, "and swindled Alec Virgil out of his stuffed wolf."

Clermont became frightened when he saw how much they knew. "I promise you I will make amends," he pleaded, "if you don't turn me in to the police."

It was clear that he was afraid of getting into trouble which might be reported to Gustav Tabor. He explained that he was the young brother of Tabor's late wife, but Gustav had never liked him. Under the old man's present will, he would inherit only a small part of the estate. He had plotted to ruin John's chances as heir in hopes of getting a larger share of the fortune himself. Instead, he might be cut out of the will altogether if Gustav learned what he was up to.

Knowing Gustav was hiring Elmo Yancey to investigate John, Clermont had flown to this country before Yancey took the case. He already was familiar with the Tabor family's werewolf tradition, and when he learned of the werewolf scare at Hawk River, he decided this would be a good way to discredit John. He had found out from local gossip about John's hospital stay and had sent an anonymous note about this to Yancey.

Frank said coldly, "Are you sure you didn't start the werewolf scare yourself?"

"No! I swear it!" the Frenchman exclaimed. On Wednesday night, he said, he had sewn straps on the wolf skin and had come to plant it on the patio of the Tabor home. Then he saw John leave the house, with Yancey trailing him and Chet trailing both of them. So he, too, had followed. After getting into a scuffle with Chet and knocking him out, he had discovered John's studio hut.

He decided the hut would be the best place to plant the wolf skin, and did so the next day. Following that he tipped off the sheriff.

"What made you trail us tonight?" Joe asked.

Clermont shrugged ruefully. "I was shadowing Yancey and saw him come to your cabin. So I wanted to find out what you two were up to and how you fitted into the picture."

"Now you know," Joe said with a dry grin.

The Hardys decided to let the Frenchman go. As an alien, he would not be hard to trace, especially since they knew his car license.

Continuing their journey, they found the rendezvous house empty. With their car parked out of sight from the road, they sat waiting for Tabor and the crooked contractor to arrive.

Suddenly a red light flashed on the radio. Chet was calling.

"What's up?" Frank asked.

"Karel Tabor and his son drove away from their house about ten or fifteen minutes ago," the boy reported. "I just got back to our place."

165

"Any idea where they were going?"

"Looked to me like they were heading north to get on Route 30," Chet replied.

"Okay, Chet. Thanks a lot," Frank said and turned off the radio.

"Route 30?" Joe muttered. "That would be in the opposite direction from here!"

A cold suspicion began forming in Frank's mind. He looked thunderstruck. "Joe! Something tells me we have been decoyed from the real action!"

"You mean Neal Xavier conned us?"

"Sure do! But he may have spun us that yarn for his boss's sake!"

"Where could the Tabors be heading, Frank?"

"If they're taking Route 30, I can only think of one place."

"Eagle's Nest!" Joe exclaimed.

"Right! Let's not waste any more time hanging around here!" Frank revved the engine and they headed back the way they had come, then swung off on a shortcut which skirted Hawk River. Soon they were rolling north on Route 30 as fast as the law would allow.

Nearing Indian Lake, they detoured to a side road and parked about a half a mile from Eagle's Nest. By approaching the site on foot through the woods, they hoped to avoid being spotted.

Joe carried a long-range walkie-talkie hooked to his belt for emergency contact with Chet. Suddenly he gripped his brother's arm. "Look!"

In a deep, wooded ravine just ahead, they glimpsed the flickering light of a concealed campfire!

"That may be the Tabors and whoever they came to meet!" Frank declared. "Come on, let's try and get close enough to see their faces!"

The boys pressed forward cautiously. As they started down into the ravine, Joe lost his footing and crashed loudly into the dry brush.

Their quarry heard the noise. Almost instantly the campfire was doused, as if smothered by dirt or a blanket. Figures burst from the little clearing and dashed off in the moon-dappled darkness.

The boys were about to give chase but stopped short with a gasp. A weird, glowing wolf-creature had just leaped into view at the bottom of the ravine! Its fangs were bared in a ferocious snarl as it charged in the Hardys' direction!

"Leaping lizards!" Joe blurted. "It's a werewolf!"

19

The Werewolf

The beast came at them like a demon of the night, its ears laid back, eyes ablaze with savagery! One glimpse of its deadly fangs told the boys they were facing a killer!

"The dart gun!" Frank cried, shaking off an instant of paralyzing fear.

They raced back to their car and around behind it. Frank unlocked the trunk, yanked out the gun, broke it open at the breech and rammed home the tranquilizing dart cartridge that Joe handed him. By now the four-legged fury was close enough to spring for his throat.

Frank whipped up the gun and fired pointblank. *Bla-a-am!* The shot thundered through the night air. He saw the creature shudder and jerk in mid-leap. Then it was upon him. He went down beneath the glowing beast, holding the gun crosswise as a barrier while he struggled to keep its jaws from his throat!

Joe grabbed the animal from behind, clutching it by the nape of the neck. The wolf-creature growled furiously as he sought to wrestle it away from his brother. But in a few moments it began to weaken from the effects of the dart anesthetic and finally it collapsed limply at their feet.

Both boys were trembling violently. It seemed a miracle that neither had been slashed by the beast's rending fangs.

"Boy, you nailed it just in time!" Joe panted.

"Look here," Frank said, pointing with the toe of his shoe toward the animal's belly. Its glowing fur appeared to be *laced up* on the underside of its body, from its throat clear back toward its tail!

For a moment Joe could only stare in amazement. "Well, for crying out loud!" he muttered.

The boys undid the lacing and, after considerable effort, managed to remove the creature's false coat. Its glowing pelt had obviously been made from synthetic fur colored with fluorescent dye and crafted with great care so as to encase the animal snugly, even including a head mask and four "leggings."

The beast itself was a huge, deep-chested Doberman pinscher!

"It's Neal Xavier's guard dog!" Frank exclaimed.

There was no time to assess their amazing discovery.

Both boys felt it was more important to find out what the campfire plotters were up to and, if necessary, thwart their latest move.

"They may be planning to ruin Eagle's Nest or wreck the restoration work somehow!" Joe conjectured.

"Could be," Frank said. "That would make *four* Chelsea building disasters. If that's their game, we've got to stop them, Joe!"

Flashlights in hand, the Hardys hurriedly retraced their steps to the ravine. Probing downward, they reached the site of the campfire and continued on past it, playing their beams cautiously right and left in hopes of picking up the fugitives' trail.

"Hold it, Joe!" Frank called out suddenly.

"What's the matter?"

"Hear that crackling noise?"

Joe listened a moment, then gasped, "Oh, oh! I sure do!"

Both boys had the same thought. A brief reconnaissance soon confirmed their fears! In their haste to douse the campfire, the fugitives had failed to extinguish it completely, and now some of the surrounding leaf litter and undergrowth had evidently caught fire from the embers! Parched from the hot, dry August weather, the brush would go up like tinder and the trees themselves would soon be ablaze!

"Good grief! We'd better get out of here, Frank!"

"You're telling me!"

170

The boys tried to run back towards their car, but found the way blocked by a wall of flames. Veering in a different direction, they sought to clamber out of the gully by one of its steeper walls. But the night breeze was spreading the blaze fast, and wherever they turned, a scorching, crackling barrier of orange-yellow flames seemed to bar their progress. Soon the whole ravine was ringed with fire!

"We're trapped!" Joe started to exclaim in despair, but he choked back the words in his throat and snatched up the walkie-talkie from his belt. He began beaming out a call to Chet, describing their horrible plight.

"Come on! Over this way, Joe!" Frank called.

Joe hurried to join him. "Where're you going?"

"There's a creek that runs through this ravine. I caught a glimpse of it in the moonlight when we were creeping up on the campfire. That'll give us a fighting chance to survive, if we can find it!"

Blundering about in the firelit darkness, the Hardys eventually reached the shallow, boggy stream. Frank had hoped that, by wading its full length, they might make their way out of the trap. But blazing trees came crashing down across the creek to block their escape. Finally they realized that their only hope was to stay hip-deep in the water and wait for rescue, or else for the fire to burn itself out.

Meanwhile, Joe continued to radio for help. But no response came over the walkie-talkie's loudspeaker.

"What's wrong? Why doesn't Chet answer?" Joe said in frustration.

"This ravine we're in or the heat waves from the fire may be interfering with our reception," Frank guessed.

"Let's hope it hasn't spoiled our transmission!"

The heat from the fire on both sides of the creek was intense. The boys splashed themselves with water to make it more bearable. Suddenly they were startled to attention by a noise from somewhere overhead.

"That's a plane, Frank!"

"I know! There it is!" The older Hardy boy pointed, "Let's try signalling with our flashlights!"

They aimed their beams skyward and waved their flashlights back and forth. Whether such feeble signals could be seen among the flames seemed doubtful, but their hopes were buoyed by the appearance of possible help.

"Look! The plane's circling, Frank!"

"The pilot must have seen us, or at least he's noticed there's a forest fire down here. Maybe *he'll* radio for help!"

What followed seemed like a miracle to the boys. A whitish stream began to spew downward from the circling aircraft. Hissing smoke billowed through the ravine as it hit the trees.

"It's chemical foam!" Frank cried joyfully.

Presently the pilot's voice came through over Joe's walkie-talkie. "Do you read me, Hardys? . . . Come in, please! . . . This is Jack Wayne in *Skyhappy Sal!*"

"We read you, Jack! And do you ever sound good!" Joe responded. "Just keep dumping that foam!"

After a few more passes by the plane, the blaze gradually sputtered out. As soon as the fire-blackened woods cooled enough underfoot to permit their passage, Frank and Joe clambered out of the ravine.

A few hundred yards beyond, they reached the road bordering Indian Lake. Ahead and to the right, they could glimpse Eagle's Nest looming on the hillside in the moonlit darkness. The boys ran toward it. Parked near the roadside was a light-colored four-door sedan. Frank and Joe recognized it as the Tabors' car, which they had seen standing in the driveway of the family's house. Something else lay on the roadway nearby.

"Frank, it's another wolf skin!" Joe exclaimed, pausing long enough to snatch it up. "Wow! Look at those fangs, and the claws feel razor-sharp!"

"This one's got straps, too, for buckling it on!" Frank noticed, playing his flashlight over the furry disguise.

"But never mind all that now, we can examine it later. Let's find out what's going on at Eagle's Nest!"

Flinging the wolf skin over the hood of the car, the Hardys hurried up the hillside. Frantic voices reached their ears.

"Help! Help!"

By this time, they were nearing the old timber mansion. Frank shone his flashlight in the direction of the cries. Two figures could be seen on the upper-story porch.

173

"It's Mr. Tabor and John! They're tied up!" Frank gasped.

The Hardys reached the building, ran inside and up a stairway. Making their way through the ancient structure, they came out on the porch and began untying the Tabors.

"The scoundrels who tied us used guns to *make* us call for help!" Karel Tabor exclaimed.

"Where are they?" Joe asked, working busily.

"You didn't see them?" put in John. "They must have gone out a different way than you came in."

At that moment they heard a resounding thud, and the whole porch quivered. More blows followed.

"Great Scott!" cried the elder Tabor. "This porch is braced with temporary supports, and they're knocking out the props with sledgehammers!"

As he spoke, there was a loud rending, creaking noise and the porch started to give way! The Hardys' hearts were in their mouths as they realized they would be dumped down the steep hillside to their deaths on the rocks far below!

20

Battle Royal

The porch swayed and teetered perilously beneath their feet. "Quick!" Frank cried. "Back inside!"

Mouldy timbers were cracking and splitting, ancient wooden pegs coming loose! Without bothering to finish untying the two prisoners, the Hardys dragged them frantically into the building through the open doorway.

Not a moment too soon! Scarcely an instant after they were inside the old mansion, a deafening *crack* resounded through the night air. The porch broke loose and crashed down the hillside!

With deft fingers, Frank and Joe finished undoing the ropes. "We'd better get out of here pronto!" Frank urged, straightening up from his task. "No telling what those crooks'll do next!"

The answer was soon apparent as the Hardys and the Tabors hurried to the stairway leading to the ground floor. Half a dozen figures were about to swarm up from below. Evidently the gang had realized that their intended victims had escaped destruction, and they were coming up to finish them off in person!

Frank and Joe recognized Neal Xavier's sharp-eyed visage among the upturned faces of their enemies, visible in the glare of the Hardys' flashlights.

"Come on! Grab some of these loose timbers!" Joe yelled to his companions.

The floor of the musty old mansion was strewn with boards, beams and other debris. Together the Hardys seized one good-sized plank and hurled it into the midst of their onrushing foes. Karel and John Tabor followed suit.

All four rained more wooden missiles on the crooks below. Then, before Xavier and his accomplices could recover their weapons and collect their wits, the group rushed down the stairway and leaped on them, kicking out and punching in all directions.

Despite the odds, the four held their own in the wild melee that followed. Even so, the outcome might have gone against them had two more fighters not joined the fray. The newcomers waded in, fists flying. One of the enemy quickly went down for keeps, then another, as punches connected with jaws. In the shadowy gloom, illuminated by moonlight streaming through the gaping windows and open sections of walls that were being replaced or repaired, Frank finally recognized their welcome allies.

"It's Dad and Jack Wayne!" he shouted to Joe.

The fight soon ended as the crooks lost heart. Neal Xavier tried to get away, but Frank brought him down with a flying tackle.

Fenton Hardy explained to his sons that he and Jack had been flying to Hawk River when they picked up Joe's radioed calls for help. Jack had landed at the airfield near Hawk River just long enough to load a tank of fire-fighting foam onto the aircraft. Then, within minutes, they had flown to the scene.

"It took a while to find a place to set down after the fire was out," Jack added, "but I guess we got here in time."

"You couldn't have timed it better!" Frank said gratefully. "Boy, that was some scrap!"

Joe was nursing a set of badly skinned knuckles. "If this joint was Dark Eagle's castle," he said with a wry chuckle, "I guess you could call what happened a battle royal!"

From among the workmen's supplies inside the mansion, Karel Tabor produced several lanterns, and Fenton Hardy proceeded to interrogate the prisoners. Besides Neal Xavier, they included the crooked contractor with whom he was involved and three of the latter's gangster stooges, as well as another man, who proved to be a male nurse from the Pine Manor Rest Home.

Mr. Tabor looked pale and exhausted from the night's hectic events. However, his color gradually returned after taking some of his heart medicine, and he seemed jubilant over the fact that the mysteries troubling his firm and his family were at last being resolved.

The Hardys learned that he had discovered several serious engineering errors in Xavier's architectural work. He also found out that Xavier had taken bribes to let the contractor use cheaper, substandard materials than the specifications called for on construction jobs which he carried out for Chelsea Builders.

"Why didn't you report him?" Fenton Hardy asked.

"I was afraid if the news leaked out it would harm our firm's good name," Karel Tabor replied. "So I agreed to say nothing if he would promise to reform and return the bribes. To ensure this, I recorded his full confession on tape."

"And that's why you said nothing when Joe and I came to your office?" put in Frank.

"Exactly. I left it to Neal's own conscience as to how much he would tell you about the stolen contents of the safe."

Xavier had cleverly twisted this situation to throw suspicion first on Upton Associates and then on his trusting boss, Karel Tabor himself, who was unaware that Xavier had, in fact, arranged the safe robbery with the help of the contractor's gangster associates in order to get rid of the incriminating tapes.

Xavier had joined Chelsea Builders with high ambitions, hoping some day to become the firm's president. Under Fenton Hardy's shrewd questioning, he confessed that he had connived with the same accomplices to cause the various building disasters and thus force Karel Tabor into early retirement.

However, John Tabor posed a new threat to his ambitions. The young architect was so brilliant, it seemed likely he would be chosen to succeed his father as head of the company. So Xavier devised the werewolf plot in order to drive the young man out of his mind, or at least make him appear unfit to run the firm.

From friendly chats with his boss, Xavier already knew about the family werewolf legend, and he gleaned other information by calling Desmond Quorn. At first he had pestered John with disturbing phone calls, disguising his voice. Later, after recommending the Pine Manor Sanatorium to the young man's father, he had harried John further with ghost voices by means of electronic gimmicks planted with the help of a friend who worked there as a male nurse. The latter was an expert hypnotist. While pretending to help John relax, the nurse had implanted post-hypnotic suggestions to make him behave suspiciously when he returned home to Hawk River.

On learning that the Tabors planned to call in the Hardy boys, Xavier had carried out the various incidents in Bayport to try and scare them off the case. He had also been the limping masquerader at the barbecue party—another step in his war of nerves against the Tabors.

Fearing that the Hardys might soon crack the case, Xavier had decided to eliminate both Karel Tabor and his son, John. To do this, he had first decoyed the Hardys off on a false scent, then lured the Tabors to Eagle's Nest with an emergency phone call.

Xavier's plan was to have his savage Doberman attack and kill the elder architect, which he assumed would not be difficult, given Tabor's weak heart. John would be found unconscious nearby with a wolf skin disguise, which Xavier had fashioned from a pelt the gangsters had stolen in a fur warehouse robbery. John would then be blamed for killing his father in a fit of werewolf mania.

"But you two punks had to spoil everything when you spotted our campfire in the ravine!" Xavier snarled at the Hardy boys.

The porch "accident" was his substitute murder plot for getting rid of all four victims, when it turned out Frank and Joe had survived the fire.

"His plan nearly worked, too," Frank remarked to his father as the Hardys strolled outside while waiting for the State Police to arrive and take charge of the prisoners.

"Another second or so, and we'd have taken a plunge with the porch," Joe added, then gasped.

"What's wrong?" Fenton Hardy inquired.

Joe hastily clambered up one of the broken porch

supports toward something that glinted in the moon-light. When he climbed down again, he was clutching a lightly gleaming hatchet.

"It's Dark Eagle's silver tomahawk!" cried Frank.

Next day, Chet and Alena accompanied the Hardy boys to the Mohawk village near Hawk River, where Frank and Joe presented the trophy to Hank Eagle. The Indians gazed at it and examined it with awed reverence.

"Dark Eagle died on the porch when he was very old, looking over the lake," Hank told the Hardys. "The mansion was probably getting pretty dilapidated even then. The tomahawk must have fallen from his hand and embedded itself in one of the supports. You don't know how much finding this means to my people!"

"It will always remind us of our proud past," said his uncle, the medicine man, "and be an inspiration to our young ones!"

"It might even inspire Chet to build a better canoe," Joe whispered to Alena with a grin.

"Listen! She's already promised to come paddling with me, wise guy!" Chet retorted. "But first we're going to stop on the way back to Hawk River for a few hamburgers and a banana split!"

You are invited to join

THE OFFICIAL NANCY DREW ®/
HARDY BOYS ® FAN CLUB!

Be the first in your neighborhood to find out about the newest adventures of Nancy, Frank, and Joe in the **Nancy Drew ®/ Hardy Boys ® Mystery Reporter,** and to receive your official membership card. Just send your name, age, address, and zip code on a postcard *only* to:

The Official Nancy Drew ®/
Hardy Boys ® Fan Club
Wanderer Books
Simon & Schuster Building
1230 Avenue of the Americas
New York, New York 10020

THE HARDY BOYS® MYSTERY STORIES
by Franklin W. Dixon

Night of the Werewolf (#59)
Mystery of the Samurai Sword (#60)
The Pentagon Spy (#61)
The Apeman's Secret (#62)
The Mummy Case (#63)
Mystery of Smugglers Cove (#64)
The Stone Idol (#65)
The Vanishing Thieves (#66)

You will also enjoy

THE TOM SWIFT® SERIES
by Victor Appleton

The City in the Stars (#1)
Terror on the Moons of Jupiter (#2)
The Alien Probe (#3)
The War in Outer Space (#4)

The Hardy Boys Mystery Series